MR. SILLY

by Roger Hargreaves

EGMONT

Mr Silly lives in Nonsenseland, which is a very funny place to live.

You see, in Nonsenseland, everything is as silly as can be.

In Nonsenseland the trees are pink!

And the grass is blue!

Isn't that silly?

In Nonsenseland dogs wear hats!

And do you know how birds fly in Nonsenseland?

No, they don't fly forwards.

They fly backwards!

It really is a very silly place indeed.

Which, of course, is why Mr Silly lives there.

Mr Silly, in fact, lives in quite the silliest-looking house you have ever seen in your whole life.

Have you ever seen a sillier-looking house than that?

Now, this particular story is all about the Nonsense Cup.

You see, in Nonsenseland each year they hold a competition, and the cup is awarded to whoever has the silliest idea of the year.

Mr Silly has never won the cup, but each night, lying in his bed, he dreamed about winning it.

In order to win the Nonsense Cup, Mr Silly realised that he would have to think up something remarkably silly.

He pondered over the problem one morning at breakfast.

Incidentally, you may be interested to know what Mr Silly was having for breakfast.

He was having a cup of coffee, which he put a spoonful of marmalade into.

After that he had a cornflake sandwich.

And to finish he had a boiled egg. But being Mr Silly, he ate the shell as well!

Isn't that a silly breakfast?

Anyway, this particular breakfast time, Mr Silly was thinking how to win that Cup.

He remembered two years ago the Cup was won by Mr Ridiculous.

He won by wallpapering his house.

Which sounds very ordinary, but in fact Mr Ridiculous had wallpapered the outside of his house!

And Mr Silly remembered last year when Mr Foolish won the Cup.

Mr Foolish, who was a friend of Mr Silly's, had won the Cup by inventing a car.

It was quite a normal car, apart from one thing. It had square wheels!

Isn't that silly?

Mr Silly thought and thought and thought, but it was no good.

He even had another cup of coffee with marmalade, but that didn't help either.

So he decided to take a walk.

Off he went, leaving his front door open so that he wouldn't have burglars when he was out.

On his walk, Mr Silly met a chicken wearing wellington boots and carrying an umbrella.

"Wouldn't it be silly if you didn't wear wellington boots and carry an umbrella?" he said to the chicken.

"Meow!" said the chicken, because animals in Nonsenseland don't make the same noises as they do in your country.

On his walk, Mr Silly met a worm wearing a top hat, a monocle and an old school tie.

"Wouldn't it be silly if you didn't wear a top hat, a monocle and an old school tie?" he said to the worm.

"Quack! Quack!" said the worm.

Next Mr Silly met a pig wearing trousers and a bowler hat.

"Wouldn't it be silly if you didn't wear trousers and a bowler hat?" he said to the pig.

"Moo!" said the pig.

Isn't that silly?

It was in the middle of Mr Silly's walk that he had his idea.

It was a beautifully silly idea.

Quite the silliest idea he'd ever had.

He hurried into town, and bought himself a pot of paint and a paintbrush.

PAI

The day of the great awarding of the Nonsense Cup arrived.

A huge crowd assembled in the City Square to see who was going to win the cup.

The King of Nonsenseland mounted the specially built platform.

"Ladies and gentlemen," he said to the crowd in the City Square. "It is my pleasure today to award the Nonsense Cup to whoever has had the silliest idea of the year."

"One of the silliest ideas of the year," continued the King, "is by Mr Muddle the farmer. He has managed to grow, of all things, a square apple!"

The crowd clapped as the square apple was held up by Mr Muddle for everybody to see.

He felt sure he was going to win.

"However," said the King, and Mr Muddle's face fell, "we have had an even sillier idea entered by Mrs Nincompoop."

It was a teapot. Quite the silliest teapot there had ever been.

The crowd broke into thunderous applause.

"I therefore have great pleasure," announced the King, "in presenting the Nonsense Cup to ..."

Just then he looked up, and stopped in astonishment.

Now, in the middle of the City Square there is a tree.

It's always been there, and it was at this tree that the King was looking in astonishment.

"What," he cried, "has happened to that tree?"

Everybody turned to look. The tree had green leaves!

Bright green leaves!

Not pink leaves like all the trees in Nonsenseland, but green.

There was an amazed silence.

"It was me," piped up Mr Silly. "I painted all the leaves green last night when you were all asleep!"

"A green tree!" exclaimed the King. "Whoever heard of a green tree?"

"A green tree!" shouted the crowd. "How silly!" And they started to applaud.

Mr Silly smiled modestly.

The King held up his hands.

"I think," he said, "that this is the silliest idea I have ever heard of, and therefore I award the Nonsense Cup to Mr Silly!"

The crowd cheered and cheered.

Mr Silly went pink with pride.

And a bird, perched high up in the branches of the silly green tree, looked down.

"Woof!" it said, and flew off, backwards!

For a long time they clung together, bodies straining to be close, their lips communicating messages of longing and desire back and forth like a heady wine being poured from one bottle to another. It felt, Lauren thought wonderingly, as if she had come in from a world of cold and darkness, to one of warmth and dazzling brightness. At last John loosened his grasp and slowly raised his head. Etched deeply in the translucent blue of his eyes was a look of such triumphant happiness that Lauren could only stare back at him, still feeling breathless and a little dizzy.

'I'd like to think of something profound to say right now,' he said huskily, 'but for the life of me I can't think of anything even intelligent.'

'Neither can I,' Lauren replied. She felt elated and terrified at the same time. Elated because she had felt an excitement that she had thought she might never feel again. Terrified because, if that excitement meant what John thought it did, it was at the wrong time, in the wrong place, and with the wrong man!

MOUNTAIN LOVESONG

BY

KATHERINE ARTHUR

MILLS & BOON LIMITED
ETON HOUSE 18-24 PARADISE ROAD
RICHMOND SURREY TW9 1SR

All the characters in this book have no existence outside the imagination of the Author, and have no relation whatsoever to anyone bearing the same name or names. They are not even distantly inspired by any individual known or unknown to the Author, and all the incidents are pure invention.

First published in Great Britain 1989
by Mills & Boon Limited

This edition 1989

ISBN 0 263 76363 3

Set in Plantin 11 on 11½ pt.
01 – 8908 – 56102

Typeset in Great Britain by JCL Graphics, Bristol

Made and Printed in Great Britain

CHAPTER ONE

'WATCH for Falling Rock'. Lauren Stanley paid scant attention to the sign, even though rocks sometimes as large as boulders did come tumbling down the moutainside on to the highway fairly often. She was too busy pleading silently with her ancient jeep to make it up the steep grade from Crook's Crossing just one more time. The jeep coughed and she shifted into a lower gear.

'Be good and I'll get you that valve job you need some day soon,' she said aloud, wondering whimsically if it was as bad policy to lie to a jeep as it was to a child. There was no way she could afford the valve job any time in the foreseeable future. In fact, she'd be lucky to meet the next mortgage payment on the lodge if business didn't pick up dramatically in the next few weeks.

She leaned forward, as if her slight weight would help the jeep's progress, ignoring the hopeful thumb stuck out in her direction by a tall, gaunt hitch-hiker, toiling up the slope with a pack on his back and a battered guitar case in one hand. He looked, Lauren thought, like an out-of-work cowboy, in that shabby western hat and boots. Those boots were hardly comfortable footwear for hiking, but they were probably all that he had. She glanced back at him briefly in her rear-view mirror. Little of his face was visible in the shade of his wide-brimmed hat, only some angular shadows above a wide, gentle mouth and a square chin that looked as if it might have a day or two's stubble of beard on it.

Probably another loser, looking for work in the timber industry, she thought with a sigh. Men who had run out of luck in other places often came to the Cascade Mountains of northern California. There was a kind of romantic appeal in lumbering, in grappling with towering Douglas firs and lodgepole pines so huge that men and their machines were dwarfed to the insignificance of ants beside them. Only a few men stayed. Lumbering was not work for the faint-hearted, nor a man who might be more comfortable taking out his guitar and singing to a tree than bucking a chain-saw against one. There was something in the hitch-hiker's slender build, his erect posture in spite of the weight of his pack, that suggested someone of artistic bent rather than a man who prided himself on his physical strength.

Lauren's mouth twisted into a wry grimace. Here she was, doing a complete character analysis on a total stranger, when she knew only too well how far off the mark she might be. She had done the same when she'd first met Paul Stanley, and had soon found out how wrong she was. Paul had been deceptively gentle-looking, but when he'd decided that Lauren was the woman for him he had swept away her reservations and captured her heart with all of the self-assured dash of a pirate subduing his lady fair.

Lauren's eyes misted over. If only Paul had been more fearful, he might still be with her. But he had taken his job as a volunteer fire-fighter very seriously, his sense of duty as strong as his courageous heart. It had done no good for her to point out on that fateful day two years ago that the forest fire that was raging was on land owned by the Redfern Timber Company; they had their own men, and they could well afford to lose a few trees. They would only cut them down later, anyway. 'The way the lightning has been and as dry as these woods are, it could happen anywhere,' Paul had said calmly, 'and we'd want them to help out if it happened here.' He had kissed her goodbye as if he were going to nothing more dangerous than a picnic. Then, that same afternoon, he had been caught beneath a falling tree . . .

The pain of his loss stabbed into Lauren's heart anew. Why? Why had Paul, of all people, been the one man who was lost? He had so much to live for—his wife, his baby son, the old resort lodge they had bought and fixed up with so much hope and optimism for the future. There hadn't been nearly enough insurance to pay off the mortgage. The Redferns, instead of offering sympathy, hadn't missed a beat in trying to take advantage of her misfortune, even though one of their own sons had disappeared from his home in San Francisco at about the same time. That event, of course, made headlines, while Paul's passing was barely noted. And it was scarcely a week after the fire when the other Redfern son, Kevin, had appeared at the lodge with an offer to buy it at what Lauren considered a pitifully low price. He had had the gall to appear annoyed that she intended to try to keep the lodge going! Just thinking about the way that weasel-faced Kevin Redfern had looked down his nose at her, as if she were an upstart serf talking back to her lord and master, still made Lauren angry. She had decided right then that pigs would fly before she sold the lodge to those disgusting Redferns, even though when business was poor she sometimes felt as if their shadows were circling overhead like vultures waiting to pounce on their prey. It wasn't fair . . .

Lauren brought herself up short, angry with herself for her lapse. Brooding, she told herself firmly, was stupid and foolish and got you nowhere. The California sun was bright, the sky was an unbelievably deep, intense blue, and there were no vultures in sight. It was, all things considered, a good day to be alive.

The road levelled out a bit. Lauren breathed a sigh of relief and picked up a little speed before she rounded the curve that signalled the beginning of the descent into Stoney Creek Canyon. The driver of a logging truck going in the other direction waved his arm energetically out of his window. Lauren smiled and waved back. When she lowered her arm, her eyes froze wide open in horror. Too late, she realised that he had not been waving. He had been signalling! Not more than fifty feet ahead of her around the curve there was a pile of rocks strewn across her side of the road, and another huge logging truck was coming towards her in the opposite direction.

'Dear heaven!' she cried, clutching the steering wheel with all of her strength and braking as rapidly as she could without skidding into the path of the oncoming truck. There was no way to escape. The jeep ploughed on to the rock pile, lurched crazily from side to side, teetered on the brink of overturning, and then righted itself on the far side with a shudder.

'We made it,' Lauren breathed, her heart racing

wildly from the burst of adrenalin the panic had given her. 'Good old jeep,' she said, bringing it to a stop and patting the steering wheel with a trembling hand. 'Good old jeep.' She sat for a moment, calming herself. That had been a close call. Much too close. Someone had better notify the highway department, so they could put up a barricade and clean up that mess before it caused a real wreck. As soon as she got back to the lodge she would call Mel Cranston and tell him. The young sheriff would know whom to call. She would omit the part about her near disaster, which was none of his business. If she did tell him, he would start clucking protectively at her, a habit which drove her to distraction.

Lauren shifted the jeep's gears into low and started up again, but she had gone only a short distance when she knew her luck had not been quite perfect. She had a flat tyre.

'Just what I need,' she muttered, frowning, her lips drawn tight in a disgusted grimace. She couldn't afford new tyres any more than she could afford the valve job. She pulled the jeep on to the shoulder of the road and stopped again, getting out to survey the damage just in time to see the right front tyre let out the last of its air with a defiant hiss. Blasted sharp rocks. She might have guessed that would happen, as old and thin as the jeep's tyres were.

'Look on the bright side,' she told herself. 'Only one is flat, and you do have a spare.' She had even been smart enough to check the air in the spare that very morning.

That thought was only briefly comforting. As Lauren pushed her grocery bags aside and pulled the jack and the lug wrench from behind the seats, she banged her left thumb, which she had hit the day before while trying to nail down a loose board on the porch of the main lodge. 'Ouch!' she said, glaring at her thumb and shaking it to ease the pain. Her ineptitude at carpentry had been a joke when she and Paul had worked together, but it was not funny any more. Especially when it looked as if she might lose her thumbnail as a result of her latest misadventure. Still frowning, she went to remove the spare tyre from its mounting on the back of the jeep.

The lug nuts holding the spare tyre in place were stuck, but Lauren managed to loosen the first two by beating on the handle of the wrench with a rock. The effort had her perspiring profusely in the hot sun, her temper growing shorter by the minute. Ordinarily she would hate falling back on the guise of a lady in distress, but right now she would be delighted if some muscular passing motorist would stop and give her a hand. Maybe if she had on a frilly dress instead of faded jeans and a T-shirt, she would have better luck. It might be a good idea to carry one along in case of emergencies. That, plus perhaps a supply of make-up and a comb to fluff up her blonde curls. Why not even some false eyelashes, too, while she was being ridiculous? she thought, smiling in amusement at the image of herself she visualised as a result. She shook her head, put the wrench on to the third bolt, and began bashing at it vigorously.

'You know, ma'am, those'd turn a sight easier if you'd oil 'em before you put 'em on,' drawled a soft, low voice behind her.

Lauren whirled around, startled, and found herself

standing face to face with the hitch-hiker. For a moment all she could do was to stare into the most intense, bright blue eyes she had ever seen, eyes that seemed to devour her with one quick glance.

'Just step aside, ma'am,' the man said, and Lauren quickly moved out of the way. He moved forward and took charge, removing the last of the nuts with a few powerful twists of the wrench, while Lauren studied him, not knowing quite what to think of this sudden answer to her prayer for assistance.

The man towered well over a foot above her own five foot two. He looked even taller and more gaunt close to, his deeply tanned cheeks hollow beneath prominent cheekbones. His hat came down on his forehead, but at the back, longish dark hair touched the collar of the plaid shirt which hung loosely from wide, square shoulders. His shirt sleeves were rolled up above his elbows, and Lauren noted that his arms did look sinewy and strong. She could easily imagine him controlling a spirited horse with those arms, and the muscular thighs that were revealed when he crouched beside her deflated tyre. What, she wondered, revising her impression that the man was a loser, was a man who was obviously a real cowboy doing hitch-hiking through the California mountains? She would have asked, but the man was so silent that she felt inhibited. In only a few minutes he had replaced the flat tyre with the spare and was inspecting the damaged tyre.

'Looks like this one's a goner,' he said, speaking again for the first time.

'Couldn't you think of something more obvious to say?' Lauren asked crossly, staring at the tyre.

Another expense. As if things weren't bad enough already. She looked up and saw that the man was frowning at her.

'I'm sorry,' she said quickly, embarrassed at taking out her ill temper on the man. 'I should be thanking you. It's just that I . . . I didn't need this particular disaster right now.'

'Not many people would,' the man observed drily. He carried the tyre to the rear of the jeep. 'These bolts are pretty rusty,' he said, as he contemplated anchoring the wrecked tyre where the spare had been. 'I don't suppose you have any oil with you, do you?'

Lauren shook her head. 'No, I'm afraid not. Just go ahead and put the nuts on a little loosely. I'll have to take it off again when I get a new tyre.'

'There's no such thing as loose with something this rusty,' the man replied. 'Pull out your dipstick. We can borrow some oil from there.'

Well! He certainly wasn't shy about ordering her around, Lauren thought. She would tell him not to bother, if it weren't such an ingenious suggestion. Instead, she gave him a reproving look before she opened the hood of the jeep and did as he suggested.

'Oil needs changing,' the man remarked, as he dribbled a few blackish drops on to the rusty bolts and then went for a second dose.

'I know,' Lauren replied, irritated at this reminder. 'And the valves need fixing and the carburettor needs something done to it, and I need new tyres, all of which cost money that I don't have right now. What else is new?'

The man gave Lauren a penetrating glance, then shrugged and tightened the tyre in its place. When he had finished, he handed the wrench to Lauren.

'All set,' he said.

'Thank you,' she responded. 'Thank you very much.' She put the wrench and the jack back into the jeep and picked up her bag. She really couldn't afford it, but she did owe the man something for his efforts. Before she could get her purse out, the man shook his head.

'No money, ma'am,' he said. 'I'm glad I could help you.'

Lauren watched him turn and pick up his pack and guitar. He looked so thin, so alone on this mountain road. He must have walked a good ten miles uphill in the sweltering July heat. There must be something she could do in return for his help. She would offer him a ride, but she wasn't going much farther.

'I—isn't there something I could do to repay you?' she asked when he turned again to face her. She felt her cheeks grow warm as an amused smile flashed briefly across the man's craggy features. 'I mean,' she said hurriedly, 'I really wish you'd take a few dollars.'

The man pushed his hat back and scratched his head thoughtfully. He gestured towards the faded lettering on the side of the jeep. 'Stoney Creek Lodge. Is that where you're going?' he asked.

'That's right,' Lauren replied. 'I own the place.'

The man raised his head and looked around him. 'Is that far from here?' he asked at last.

'Only about four miles farther,' Lauren answered. 'I'd be glad to give you a ride that far, if you'd like.'

'We-ell,' the man drawled slowly, 'I was wondering if you've got some odd jobs that need doing? I'd be glad to work for my room and board as long as I could be useful. Or does your husband have things pretty well fixed up?'

'My—my husband?' Lauren asked numbly, still feeling a sharp stab of pain at those words.

The man looked at her curiously. 'You are wearing a wedding ring,' he said.

'Oh. Oh, yes,' Lauren said, looking down at the simple gold band. She shook her head and blinked rapidly to clear her eyes. 'I don't have a husband. He—he was killed about two years ago, fighting a forest fire. I haven't taken my ring off, because I don't plan to marry again.'

'Oh, ma'am, I am so deeply sorry,' the man said, the intensity of his voice making Lauren look up at him quickly. She saw the pain she felt reflected like a mirror in his eyes, almost as if he felt it too. 'Did it happen nearby?' he asked. 'It seems to me I remember hearing of some fires in this area about that time.'

Lauren nodded. 'Only about a mile from the lodge, on the other side of the canyon,' she replied huskily. 'If it had been farther away, I might have persuaded him not to go.'

'Perhaps not,' the man said softly. 'Some men feel it's their duty to help save the forests.'

'Paul did,' Lauren agreed with a sigh. Her mouth tightened angrily. 'But it wasn't the national forest, it all belonged to the Redfern Timber Company! And they didn't even . . .' She stopped herself. That was not something to talk to this stranger about. 'Never mind,' she said, as he looked at her questioningly. 'It's not your problem.' Right now she needed to decide whether to take his offer of assistance. Her forehead puckered as she looked at the man and he returned her gaze unflinchingly. He had a kind face. He seemed trustworthy. She did have a lot of odd jobs that needed doing, but she knew nothing about him except that he had changed her tyre very skilfully. He seemed to read her thoughts.

'A woman alone has to be careful,' he said, 'and you don't know anything about me. My name's John Smith, and I've been cowboying in Texas for a couple of years, but I've done some construction work, too.' He reached into his hip pocket and held out a plastic-covered card. 'I know that a driver's licence doesn't prove anything, but it's the only identification I've got. But I can assure you I'm an honest man, and don't have any criminal record of any kind.'

Lauren looked at the licence. 'John Smith,' she said aloud, still hesitant. 'I don't think I've ever met anyone who was really named John Smith before.'

John Smith chuckled. 'Somebody's got to be John Smith. They can't all be fictitious. Tell you what, ma'am, you can try me out, and if my work isn't satisfactory, I'll just be on my way again. But I don't think you'll be disappointed. I can do carpentry, plumbing, electrical work. Whatever you need. I might even be able to help your old jeep a little.'

That, Lauren thought, sounded almost too good to be true. Well, why not? 'All right, Mr Smith,' she said. 'I'll give you a try. By the way, my name is Lauren Stanley. Hop in. I'm afraid my groceries shouldn't have been sitting out in the heat this long.'

'Yes, ma'am . . . Mrs Stanley. Thank you.'

John Smith stowed his gear in the jeep and then folded his length into the seat. Lauren got in and reached for her seat-belt. Her injured thumb banged against the side of the car.

'Ouch! Darned thumb,' she said, frowning at it. She held it out as John bent towards her to look at the source of her complaint. 'I hit it with a hammer, trying to nail down a board on the lodge porch yesterday,' she explained.

'Looks like fate sent me here about a day too late for that thumb,' John said with a rueful smile. He took hold of her hand and inspected her thumb more closely. 'You may lose that thumbnail.'

'I'm afraid so,' Lauren agreed, feeling a strange little shiver go through her at the touch of his long, slender fingers. Odd that he should mention fate. She had been in desperate need of someone to make some repairs at the lodge. Had providence sent this lonesome hitch-hiker to her rescue, even putting those rocks in her path to force her to stop so that they would meet? No, of course not. That was silly. It was only a lucky coincidence. Besides, it remained to be seen if he was as good as he said he was. He might just move in and then lie around, plucking his guitar. If he tried that, she would send him on his way in a hurry. She set the jeep in motion.

'Tell me, Mr Smith,' she said, 'how you happen to be in California? You sound as if you've been in Texas all of your life.'

'Call me John, Mrs Stanley,' he said. 'Actually, I'm a Californian. I guess I picked up the drawl from the other cowhands. It'll probably wear off after a while.'

'How long were you in Texas?' Lauren asked.

'A couple of years. I was doing the constructoin work I mentioned before that, on a big shopping centre south of San Francisco. When that ended, I hitched a ride with a trucker who turned out to be going to Texas. I guess I always wanted to be a cowboy, so I took that as an omen. Had the trucker let me out at the first ranch gate we passed.' John paused and chuckled. 'It was a good five miles back to the house, but I was in luck. They needed some hands, so I stayed. I never regretted it for a minute, either.'

'Then why did you leave?' Lauren asked. 'Didn't they need you any more?'

'The rancher sold out and retired,' John replied. 'I thought I'd come back and tie up some loose ends in California before I decided what to do next.' He looked out at the tree-covered slopes beside them. 'I think I'm going to enjoy it up here. I'd forgotten how beautiful the Cascade Mountains are. It's very different from the dry and dusty spaces where I've been.'

'They are lovely,' Lauren agreed. Sometimes lately she had forgotton how much she loved these mountains. Maybe, with John Smith to help out, she might have time to appreciate them once in a while. The only fly in the ointment would be Mel Cranston. Since Paul had died, he seemed to think he was next in line for her hand, even though she had made it abundantly clear that she was not looking for a 'next' husband. He was not going to take kindly to her having another man around Stoney Creek Lodge, especially one as attractive as John Smith.

For John was attractive, in a very strong and masculine way. He had taken off his hat, revealing thick, wavy dark brown hair that covered the nape of his neck and lent the only softness to his sharply angular features. Mel would hate that hair, too. He favoured only very short, military haircuts, and frequently told her that her son Brian's hair was too long. As for Brian, it was going to be interesting to see how he reacted to John. She knew he did not like Mel Cranston very much.

'I should warn you,' Lauren said, 'that you'll probably have a four-year-old helper part of the time. My son Brian. He likes to try everything I do.'

'That's no problem,' John said quickly. 'I like kids. There was a little fellow at the ranch who followed me everywhere. He got to be a pretty good fence-fixer before I left.'

Somehow, Lauren thought, she would have expected John to like children. 'You'd better not tell Brian how you got to be a cowboy,' she said, 'or he's apt to start hitch-hiking for Texas. There's nothing he'd like better than to be a cowboy.'

Just then they drew even with the small sign that announced Stoney Creek Lodge, an arrow pointing down the gravel road on to which Lauren turned the jeep.

'Your sign needs repainting,' John said. 'So does the lettering on the jeep. Do you have some paint?'

Lauren frowned. 'Well . . . yes, I think so,' she answered, 'but those aren't on my critical list.'

'First impressions are important in business,' John contradicted her firmly. 'I'll take care of that sign this evening.'

'I hadn't planned on putting you to work until tomorrow,' Lauren said, rather annoyed by the way he seemed to think he could move right in and make his own rules. It was, after all, her lodge. 'Besides, I'm not sure I want that done right away,' she added. 'We might miss some guests if the sign is down.'

'I doubt it attracts many people, the shape it's in, but I'll take it down after ten and have it back up by dawn,' John replied unruffled.

'That's ridiculous,' Lauren said sharply, feeling insulted by his appraisal of her sign. 'You have to sleep. It takes time to do good lettering.'

John smiled. 'Don't worry, I'll get enough sleep. I've done lettering before.'

'Is there anything you haven't done?' Lauren asked testily as she turned into the drive that circled in front of the rustic lodge building, its long, low shape sheltered and shaded by a stand of venerable pines.

'Never had to argue with a boss about whether I'd get enough sleep or not,' John answered. 'Beautiful place,' he added as Lauren stopped the jeep.

Immediately a small boy burst through the screened door and came running down the steps of the lodge porch, his blond hair flopping over his forehead as he ran, a beagle at his heels.

'Mommy, Mommy!' he cried, flinging himself at her and clinging as she swept him into her arms. 'There's some people here from Pennsylvania, and they're going to stay in the big cabin a whole week!'

'Terrific!' Lauren said, giving him a hug and a kiss.

'Who's that?' Brian demanded, as John Smith got out of the jeep, and reached down and patted the dog, who wagged his tail vigorously. 'Hey, look, Frank likes him.'

'My name's John,' he said, looking up, 'and I gather this is Frank. You must be Brian. Your mother said you're a pretty good carpenter's helper.'

'Yeah,' Brian said, looking John over carefully. He

looked at Lauren. 'Is he going to fix stuff for us?'

'That's right,' Lauren answered, putting the boy down. 'Say "how do you do" to Mr John Smith, Brian.' She watched as Brian gravely repeated her words and stuck his small hand out, and John Smith bent and gave him an equally polite greeting, engulfing the boy's small hand in his huge, long-fingered one. Then she burst out laughing as Brian volunteered in his high little voice, 'We sure do need you around here. Mommy's an awful carpenter.'

John nodded in agreement. 'I know. I've seen her thumb,' he said. 'Shall we help her carry in the groceries?'

John Smith was too good to be true, Lauren thought, watching him hand Brian a bag of oranges to carry. He was a natural with children, unlike Mel, who tended to be entirely too hearty and patronising.

They carried a load of groceries into the lodge kitchen, and Lauren introduced John to Isobel Minnick, the motherly woman who cooked for the lodge guests and helped Lauren with the cleaning.

Isobel looked John over sceptically and then asked bluntly, 'You don't eat weird food, do you?'

'No, ma'am,' John replied with a smile. 'I like most everything.'

'Good. We'll fatten you up a bit, then,' Isobel said. 'You're too thin.'

'I don't think she'll have much luck,' John commented as they went for another load of groceries. 'I've always been thin.'

'You'd better try,' Lauren said, 'or Isobel will go into a depression. She puts her whole heart and soul into her cooking. Oh, no. Frank, come back here!'

The dog had gone tearing past them, barking ferociously at the police car coming to a stop behind the jeep. Mel Cranston would pick this time to show up, Lauren thought unhappily. She had hoped to have the rest of this day to get John settled in before she had to cope with explaining him to Mel. 'It's a friend of mine,' she explained hurriedly, as Mel got out of his car and frowned at the dog, who backed off sullenly. 'Hi, Mel!' she said, giving the officer a little wave. 'Your timing is perfect. I've someone I want you to meet.'

Mel Cranston, his uniform shirt tight across his barrel chest, strode towards them, looking from Lauren to John Smith with a questioning frown on his round face. 'What's up?' he asked.

'This is John Smith,' Lauren replied. 'He's going to do some repair work for me in exchange for room and board. John, this is Mel Cranston, an old friend of Paul's and mine.'

The two men shook hands, Mel surveying the taller man warily. 'Where you from, Smith?' he asked.

'Texas, most recently,' John replied. 'The Bar-C ranch.'

'Where did you find him?' Mel demanded of Lauren. 'I don't remember any John Smiths looking for work around here.'

'He stopped to help me change a tyre,' Lauren answered, feeling the tension building in the air. Mel, she knew, would want to know every detail about John, partly out of a misguided desire to protect her, and partly from an equally misguided desire to protect his own interests.

Mel planted his hands on his hips and looked

around. 'Where's his car?'

'I don't have one,' John answered, before Lauren could speak. 'I was hitch-hiking.'

'Hitch-hiking!' Mel stared incredulously at Lauren. 'You mean you brought some hitch-hiker home with you, with little Brian here and all? Haven't you got any sense?'

'Mel,' Lauren said, trying to keep the irritation from her voice, 'I gave Mr Smith a pretty good third degree myself before I did. I'm quite sure he's all right, and you know how much I need some help around the place.'

'You are just so naïve, it's pitiful,' Mel said, giving John Smith a look which plainly said he thought him some kind of criminal. 'Let's see some identification,' he said to John. 'I'll bet you haven't even got a driver's licence, have you?'

John Smith silently reached into the back pocket of his jeans and handed his licence over to Mel, who took it and stared at it suspiciously.

'Texas, huh? I'll just check this out.' He started for his car, and the two-way radio that would put him in touch with the computerised data system.

'Why don't you do something useful instead? There's a rock-slide about four miles away down the road that needs clearing off,' Lauren snapped, feeling an almost unbearable combination of anger and anxiety. What if it turned out that John was wanted for some crime? Most confusing of all, if he was, she wasn't sure whether she'd feel more miserable about her bad judgement or about John's being found out.

'That slide's already been reported,' Mel answered, opening his car and slipping inside.

Lauren bit her lip and looked up at John. He gave her a comforting wink. A few minutes later Mel returned.

'Well, he isn't wanted for anything . . . yet,' he said, handing John his licence. 'But you'd better toe the straight and narrow while you're here,' he added warningly. He redirected his gaze to Lauren. 'Where are you going to put him up?'

'I haven't got to that yet,' Lauren replied. 'We've only just got here.'

'Why don't you put him in that burnt-out cabin?' Mel suggested. 'That ought to be good enough for someone like him.'

Lauren was so close to reaching out and slapping Mel as hard as she could that she was momentarily speechless.

'Burnt-out cabin?' John said in a soft, calm voice.

'Yes.' Lauren nodded, trying to mimic his calmness. 'It is our nicest one. We had some honeymooners in there who forgot something on the stove. It's a mess. There hasn't been anyone in there in . . . two years.'

Brian, who had been watching the clash between the adults with wide, unhappy eyes, piped up, 'You want to see it?' to John. 'Come on, I'll show you.'

John looked at Lauren questioningly.

'Go ahead,' she said. She watched as Brian took John's hand and led him off on the path to the secluded cabin set back among the pines, then turned back to Mel. 'Mel Cranston,' she said, her voice quivering with emotion, 'your behaviour towards Mr Smith is unforgivable. You have no reason to treat him like some kind of derelict. A man is innocent until he's proven guilty, not the other way around. Or don't you believe in our Constitution any more?' She knew that that last would hit Mel where he was most vulnerable, for he prided himself on being a staunch defender of citizens' rights.

Mel grimaced. 'It's not the same when someone you care about might be in danger,' he said. 'Just because you picked up some stray, don't go getting Constitutional with me. I don't like the man's looks. He's got a hungry look about him.'

'Well, he probably is hungry!' Lauren almost shouted. 'Why don't you go back and save the rest of the county and stop bothering me?'

'Now, sweetheart, don't get upset,' Mel said, smiling cajolingly. 'I wasn't talking about the man's being hungry for food, if you know what I mean. It's the way he was looking at you.'

'You're imagining things, Mel,' Lauren said coldly. She had known he would be jealous. If any of the male guests even smiled at her when he was around, he would remark on it later. 'Now, if you don't mind, I've got a million things to do. We've got some people from Pennsylvania staying for a week, and I haven't even met them yet, much less found out how many there are and what kind of menus to plan.'

'OK,' Mel shrugged, 'but keep a sharp eye on your Mr Smith. I'll stop by in the morning and make sure everything's al right.'

Lauren wanted to tell him that if he did she'd throw something at him, but knew that that would only increase his suspicions. She smiled weakly instead. 'Thanks, Mel,' she said. 'Be careful out there.'

'Yes, ma'am,' he said, giving her a salute. 'I always am.'

John and Brian returned just after Mel had driven away.

'I think your friend is right,' John said. 'That cabin is perfect for someone like me.'

'Oh, for heaven's sake!' Lauren said, scowling at him. 'It is not! It would take days to get it cleaned up enough . . .'

'Which I will do,' John said. 'Don't argue.'

'Don't argue? I'll argue if I want to! It isn't fit . . .' Lauren spluttered to a stop. Where did John Smith get the idea that he could order her around? And what was it about him that made her feel as if she ought to listen to what he said? She was going to have to establish the fact that she was running things. If he thought he could take over the lodge repairs the way he had taken over changing her tyre . . . 'I don't have time to argue now, but I will later,' she said, lifting her chin and giving him a defiant scowl. 'Brian, why don't you show John around and then take him to one of the lodge rooms so he can get cleaned up for dinner? We'll eat at six.'

'C'mon,' Brian said happily. 'I'll show you Horse.'

'Horse?' John raised his eyebrows and looked questioningly at Lauren.

'That's what Brian named him when he was two,' Lauren said. 'He's a useless old hay-burner, but Brian loves him.'

With that, Lauren turned and went into the lodge, wondering why she felt perfectly secure in leaving the most precious thing in her life, Brian, in the company of John Smith. Brian had certainly taken to the tall, quiet man, but he was only a child. Was she, as Mel had said, being terribly naïve? She shook her head.

No, she didn't think so. John seemed to her to be exactly what he appeared to be: a person who had worked at many different jobs but had no interest in acquiring more possessions than he could carry with him. But was that really all that he was? The soft way he spoke, the almost aristocratic way he carried himself, with his head held high and his shoulders back, suggested someone of a more elegant background than would be expected of an itinerant worker. It made her rather curious. Perhaps some time she would ask him, if he stayed long enough.

Lauren showered quickly and put on some of her nicer slacks and a pale yellow blouse which almost matched her hair. She would be on duty as waitress during dinner, as usual, and wanted to look as nice as possible for the guests. And John Smith? suggested some brash little imp from a dark corner of her mind. Of course not. She always dressed up a little for dinner, and the eyeshadow and mascara helped to cover the slight puffiness in her eyelids that her allergies caused.

There were scheduled to be eight people for dinner tonight, besides herself, John, Brian and Isobel. The group from Pennsylvania, two middle-aged brothers and their wives, had said they'd prefer dining at the lodge to cooking in their cabin, and the two young couples who were in rooms in the main lodge were eating in tonight also. Before she left her room, Lauren glanced out of the window hopefully as she always did, wishing fervently for some additional guests. This time, just as she did, a large van appeared as if by magic from behind the cluster of pines which hid the entrance to the drive. It stopped, and a family of two adults and four children tumbled out.

'Good heavens!' Lauren muttered. 'This must be my lucky day.' She hurried to the little registration foyer between the dining-room and lounge just in time to greet the group. They were tired, hungry and thoroughly delighted with the cabin that Lauren showed them, with its view overlooking the canyon and creek below. With a fervent prayer that Isobel would be up to this challenge, Lauren hurried back to the lodge to set the tables for dinner. What she saw when she reached the dining-room made her stop and stare in amazement. John, clean-shaven, his dark hair still damp from a shower and neatly combed, and now wearing a very presentable blue western shirt and newer jeans, was supervising Brian setting the tables.

'Am I doing it right, Mommy?' Brian asked, spotting her and smiling happily. 'John says I am.'

'That's just fine,' Lauren replied. 'You'll have to set the big round table, too. There'll be six more coming.'

Brian hurried to the silverware cabinet, and Lauren walked over to John's side. 'I . . . er . . . don't expect you to work all the time,' she said.

John lifted one eyebrow and gave Lauren a penetrating glance. 'Is this work? I didn't know that,' he said, a flicker of amusement in his eyes.

Lauren looked away, feeling uncomfortable. 'Well, most people would think it is,' she said. But then, it was becoming obvious that John Smith was definitely not most people. She looked back, to see him smiling, as if he knew what she was thinking and it amused him. 'Go ahead and have fun, then, or whatever,' she said, and hurried off before the warmth she felt in her cheeks could turn into a real blush. There was something about that man that made her nervous. Maybe it was the way he usually smiled with his lips closed that did it. It added to his mysterious air, as if a broad grin would let something out that he wanted to keep inside.

'Can we cope all right?' Lauren asked Isobel, when she had informed her of the new arrivals.

'Oh, sure,' said Isobel calmly. 'That is, if everyone doesn't want the same thing. But the kids will probably want hamburgers.'

The guests had just begun arriving in the dining-room when another car drove up, this time with a lone man.

Lauren hesitated, momentarily torn between delivering water to the diners and registering the man. John immediately saw her plight.

'May I?' he asked. He did not wait for an answer, but took the tray of water glasses from Lauren's hands and picked up the order pad.

'I . . . suppose so,' she said, hesitantly, but he had already gone through the door. She looked at Isobel and shrugged, then went to greet the new arrival. She was going to have to straighten some things out with John, she could see that. Just because he could do anything, didn't mean she wanted him to. But then, maybe after a few days his enthusiasm would wane. First impressions were important, he had said that himself. Well, he certainly knew how to impress an employer with his industry, and she might as well be glad he wanted to help out tonight. Fifteen for dinner was a lot more than usual.

Lauren was even more glad of John's help later, for the four children were decidedly unruly. He moved among the tables, gracious and unruffled, as if he had at some time served dinner to the very wealthy. Maybe, Lauren thought with a sigh, he had done that, too. He looked to be in his mid-thirties. Time enough to have tried dozens of different jobs. Still, she had hired him to do repair work.

'I appreciate your help tonight,' she told him when the guests had left, 'but I don't expect you to do it every night. It wouldn't be fair.'

He looked down at her in that way she had discovered he had of dropping his heavily fringed eyelids without bending his neck. It gave him an almost haughty appearance. 'Let me decide about that,' he said in a manner which left no room for argument. 'I'll help whenever I'm needed.'

'I doubt that will be very often,' Lauren replied, in an attempt to respond without appearing to back down completely. But, when he even tried to give her the tips he had received, she balked.

'You earned it, you keep it,' she told him firmly. When he frowned, she glared at him. 'Don't you dare argue,' she said, using his own threat against him. 'And don't think you're going to help with the dishes, either,' she added, as he ignored her instructions, put the money down on the long counter, and started for the sink. 'Isobel and I will do them after I put Brian to bed. You sit down and have the last of that cherry pie.'

John stopped and looked over his shoulder at Lauren.

'*After* the dishes are done,' he said firmly. 'Why don't you just run along and put Brian to bed?'

'Just . . . run along?' Lauren spluttered, planting her

hands on her hips. Her voice rose. 'Do you mind if I give the orders around here?' She looked around as Isobel coughed uncomfortably. Brian was also staring at her curiously.

'Why can't he help with the dishes, Mommy?' he asked. 'He's big enough, isn't he?'

Out of the corner of her eye, Lauren could see John smiling again. 'Yes, of course he is,' she answered. 'It's just that I thought he might be tired.'

'Are you tired?' Brian asked, looking at John.

John nodded. 'But so is your mother. I think that's the reason she's cross.'

Lauren opened her mouth to begin a denial, then closed it as Brian nodded sagely and said, 'Yeah, she gets that way sometimes.'

'All right, I give up,' Lauren said with a sigh. 'Come on, Brian. Finish your milk.'

'Yuk,' said Brian, but he downed his milk and carried the glass to the sink. 'Will you come and say goodnight to me?' he asked John.

'Sure thing,' John agreed.

Lauren took Brian across the lounge area and down the short hallway to their little apartment, feeling troubled. She had wanted Brian to get along with John, but she didn't want him getting too fond of the man. It would be that much harder for him when John went on his way again, as he doubtless would. But how could she explain something like that to a four-year-old? When Brian was bathed and in his pyjamas he went scampering back to the kitchen to get John, his enthusiasm apparent. He came back riding piggy-back, giggling happily as John set him carefully on his bed. Lauren tucked the covers around him and gave him a kiss on his soft, warm cheek.

'Goodnight, love,' she said. 'Sleep tight.'

'G'night, Mommy,' Brian said. He held his arms up towards John, who hesitated only a moment and then bent and gave the boy a warm hug and a kiss.

As she watched them, an ache formed in Lauren's heart. Brian had obviously been taken with John at first sight, and it looked as though John might feel the same way, too. Should she, perhaps, send John Smith away, before it became too difficult to do?

'Pleasant dreams, Tiger,' John said, and Brian giggled again and then made a growling sound.

'I'm not a real tiger,' he said.

'Close enough,' John replied. 'See you in the morning.'

Lauren said very little, lost in thought, as the dishes were finished and put away. She really should send John away before Brian got too attached to him. He was definitely not husband material . . . if she were looking for a husband, which she wasn't. The only thing that could possibly persuade her to risk marrying again would be if a knight in shining armour with a full wallet were to come riding to her rescue, whisking her away to a world of luxury and privilege where she never had to worry about a mortgage payment again. The last thing she needed or wanted was a man who had no steady income, no ambition to get ahead in the world. But whenever she looked at John, working quietly and efficiently beside her, she could not imagine how she could tell him to go. Somehow, she knew he would, if she asked. He would simply pack up his little store of belongings and walk back out of her life forever. For some silly reason, that thought brought a mist to her eyes. It returned when, after Isobel had retired to her room, John seemed to have read her thoughts.

'Would you rather I didn't stay?' he asked, his voice especially soft and low.

'No, why?' Lauren denied immediately.

'Something's bothering you,' John said. 'I thought perhaps you were having second thoughts. I'd understand, what with Brian liking me so well, and your friend Mel obviously not. I don't want to create problems for you instead of helping.'

Lauren bit her lip, feeling almost lost in the intense blue of John's eyes as he watched her. It was uncanny. No one was that thoughtful, that perceptive. He needed the job. Didn't he? She stared so long into John's eyes that she began to feel dizzy.

'D-don't you want to stay?' she faltered.

'Very much,' John replied.

'Then do,' Lauren said quickly. She rubbed her hand across her tired eyes. 'I'll handle Brian, and Mel doesn't count. Now, about where you're going to stay . . .'

'That cabin isn't too bad,' John broke in quickly, apparently accepting her answer, 'and I'd really prefer to be away from the lodge so that I can play my guitar at night without bothering anyone. I'll sleep in my bedroll until I get things cleaned up enough for sheets on the bed. The bedroom was hardly touched by the fire, and the mattress seems all right. I should be able to use it by tomorrow. If you've got a lantern you can give me for tonight, I'll borrow the jeep and pick up the sign as I go.'

'All right,' Lauren said with a sigh, seeing that argument with John would be useless, as usual. 'But would you *please* let that sign go until tomorrow night? I haven't had time to look for the paint.'

John smiled, that amused smile again. 'Yes, ma'am,' he said. 'If I don't have to get the sign, I can walk.'

'I'll drive you,' Lauren said firmly. 'I want to see how bad the place is and take some cleaning supplies up there. Get your things and I'll meet you out front.' She might be tired, but she was not going to have John Smith sleeping in piles of litter and debris. She seemed to remember that some pieces of the ceiling had fallen on the floor. She gathered up broom and dustpan and some bags for the rubbish, and two camping lanterns, and stowed them into the jeep just as John appeared.

'Good idea,' he said upon seeing them. 'I'll get the electricity and water working again as soon as possible. By the time I leave, I'll have the place usable again.'

'I don't see how,' Lauren commented a few minutes later, when they were in the cabin, the bright lanterns illuminating the charred streaks on the walls. 'It will take a lot of materials I'm not sure I can afford.'

'I'll find a way,' John said with a shrug.

Lauren studied him thoughtfully as he stood with his hands planted on his hips, surveying the room. He seemed so confident, so competent. There was nothing about him, except for his life-style, that suggested a man lacking in ambition or purpose.

'Have you always just gone from job to job?' she asked.

John shook his head. 'No. Not always,' he replied.

He turned his intense blue gaze on Lauren and changed the subject abruptly. 'If you don't mind my asking,' he said, 'why did you say that Mel doesn't count? I had the impression that he thought he did.'

That, Lauren thought, was a rather personal question. Still, she had made the remark, so she supposed she could explain it. 'He does think that,' she replied with a grimace. 'But he's only a friend, as I've tried to tell him many times. He just won't listen. He insists that some day I'll see the light and marry him.'

'Perhaps you will,' John said, 'if you haven't been able to give him any good reasons why you won't.'

Lauren's eyes widened. 'Well, I can't give him the most important one,' she said. 'Brian detests him, and he's too dense even to see it. And I certainly don't love him. Even if I did, I'd be very reluctant to marry someone in as dangerous a line of work as law enforcement. I'd never sleep a wink, worrying. And if I ever do think of marrying again, it's going to be to someone with a reasonable amount of money. It may not buy happiness, but this hovering on the edge of bankruptcy isn't much fun either.'

John gave her a sideways look. 'At least you have a beautiful place to hover in. I like the way you've kept it so natural and unspoiled.'

'That's the way I want to keep it,' Lauren said. She sighed heavily. 'Mel thinks I'm crazy not to sell out to the Redferns, but . . .' She shook her head. 'I don't want to think about that tonight. Every time I do, I get upset.' She looked up at John, who was frowning. 'What's wrong?' she asked.

'I thought you said the Redferns were in the timber business,' he replied. 'Surely they don't want your place for the timber. How much land do you have?'

'Forty acres. No, they don't want the timber. They've branched out into the resort business in the last couple of years. This is a prime location, with the stream running through it and the highway nearby. They want to build a fancy, expensive place with a swimming pool and tennis courts. I suppose it's all right, but there aren't many places for families who can't afford such things any more. If I can't hold out, there won't be any around here.' She grimaced. 'I'd better start on this mess. I should have done it a long time ago.' She picked up the broom. John immediately put his hand on the broom also, and shook his head.

'Let me do it,' he said. 'You're tired.'

'I'm not that tired,' Lauren said stubbornly. She frowned. 'Stop that,' she said, as John carefully pried her fingers from the broom, and then held her hand in his.

'You're almost bleary-eyed,' he said, his smile warm and gentle. 'Now be a good girl and run along to bed. I want to see you looking bright and beautiful in the morning. By the way, is it all right if I take Horse out for a ride early in the morning? The old fellow could use some working out.'

'Of course,' Lauren replied, nodding.

'Thank you,' John said.

Then, while Lauren watched with a feeling of unreality, her heart beating faster every second, John raised her hand, uncurled her clenched fingers, kissed the palm of her hand, and then tucked her fingers tight again. He stared into her eyes for a moment, as if seeking something, then smiled again.

'Goodnight, Lauren,' he said.

'G-goodnight,' Lauren stammered, her heart still

pounding. She turned and walked from the cabin as if in a trance, already sleepwalking, and got into the jeep. Her hand was still clenched tightly, the imprint of the touch of John's lips as vivid as if he had left a part of himself there. She opened her hand and stared at it, reluctant to touch it to the cold steering wheel. Instead, she closed it again, and drove back to the lodge with it still clenched, feeling vaguely foolish but unable to do differently.

Once inside her room, she sat on the edge of her bed and looked at her hand again. In the light, it looked as clean and untouched as her other hand, but it still felt very different, as if it were tingling in some kind of anticipation.

'You're being ridiculous,' Lauren scolded herself. Maybe if she washed the hand it would get her over this nonsense. She did so, scrubbing it thoroughly. She brushed her teeth, put on her pyjamas, and got into bed, tucking her hand beneath her pillow. It lay there, the palm feeling warm and vibrant, unmoved by her efforts to squelch the notion that tickled at the edges of her mind. At last Lauren groaned, pulled the hand from under the pillow, and pressed it to her lips. Immediately, a great wave of longing swept through her and she burrowed into her pillows, imagining John's arms around her, his lips possessing hers with a passionate kiss. It was several minutes before she could wrench herself back to reality.

'Oh, lord,' she said, tears springing to her eyes, 'this can't be happening to me!' John was only a handyman. In the morning, she would have to speak to him about being so forward. He had even called her Lauren without asking her permission. She did not like it. She didn't like it at all!

CHAPTER TWO

LAUREN was up at six a.m. feeling tired and cross. She had spent a large part of the night arguing with herself over her strong reaction to John Smith. Just because Mel called forth no physical reaction, she shouldn't be so surprised. At twenty-six, her hormones had scarcely stopped functioning, and she would be unrealistic to expect to live another sixty years or so without finding any man attractive. It must be simply the result of two years without any close contact with a physically attractive man. John was tall and handsome and mysteriously romantic-looking. She had best keep in mind that he was nothing more than an itinerant handyman, who doubtless took love wherever he could find it. Rather than scolding him, it would probably be best to say nothing at all about his little kiss on her hand, or he would know how much it had bothered her. He already seemed very good at reading her thoughts. In spite of her sleep-deprived brain feeling like a bowl of hot mush, she would have to be bright and chipper this morning, or he would jump to entirely the wrong conclusions.

She dressed and went into Brian's room to waken him. The little boy was already gone, his pyjamas lying in a heap on the floor. Already off to find John Smith, I'll bet, Lauren thought grimly. Somehow she was going to have to convey the idea to Brian that John was not going to be a permanent fixture at Stoney Creek Lodge. Perhaps the best approach would be to make a list of the things she would ask John to do before he went on his way. Then, as she checked them off, Brian would be able to see that John's time with them was coming to a close. First of all, though, she had better look for Brian and be sure he was all right. For all she knew, John Smith could be a Jekyll and Hyde type—charming one day and cruel the next.

That thought sent a shiver through Lauren. She hurriedly checked the kitchen, but Isobel had seen neither Brian nor John yet.

'I don't think you need to fret,' Isobel said, seeing Lauren's anxious look. 'John Smith looks like a regular angel in disguise to me.'

'Maybe,' Lauren said, feeling a strange tingle at Isobel's mention of a disguise. Apparently she, too, had the impression that there was more to John Smith than met the eye. 'I'd better see if Brian's playing human alarm clock. I forgot to tell him not to bother Mr Smith too early.'

Lauren tried to stroll casually up the pine-needle-covered path to John's cabin, but her heart insisted on skipping and pounding as if she were about to go on stage and didn't know her lines.

'Brian . . . John,' she called as lightly as she could manage when she reached the porch of the cabin. A silence that seemed suddenly ominous greeted her call. Anxiety now making her pulse beat even faster, she pounded vigorously on the door. There was still no answer. She threw the door open. The room was empty, but John's bedroll was lying on the now clean floor. Where could he have gone? Where had he taken Brian?

In a near panic, she ran back outside. The distant sound of Horse whinnying made her stop. Of course! He'd taken Brian riding with him! She hurried down the path to the stable, just in time to see John riding up to the paddock gate. He was alone.

'Where's Brian?' Lauren demanded, her heart suddenly racing again.

'I haven't seen him,' John replied. He bent his head and peered at Lauren's anxious face. 'What's wrong, Lauren? Is he missing?'

'Yes. He got dressed and went out before I was up. I—I thought maybe he was with you.'

John's eyes narrowed. He swung down from Horse and stood in front of Lauren, fixing her with an intent stare. 'I haven't seen him,' he repeated in precise, clipped syllables. 'For goodness' sake, Lauren, what kind of a monster do you think I am?'

Lauren bit her lip, suddenly feeling very foolish. Mel and his blasted suspicions! He had her imagining things that were absolutely ridiculous, and now she had hurt John's feelings. 'I don't think you're a monster at all,' she denied. 'I'm just worried!'

'Mmm-hmm,' John said sceptically, raising one eyebrow. 'Come on, let's go find him. Get on the horse first and I'll get up behind you.' When Lauren hesitated, he impatiently grabbed her beneath her armpits and hoisted her bodily into the saddle. Then he swung up behind her, reached around her, and took the reins. 'I've been uphill from here and I didn't see Brian,' he said, his voice very close to Lauren's ear. 'Where else might he be?'

'He might have gone down to the creek,' Lauren replied. 'He knows he isn't supposed to go there alone, though.'

'Let's take a look,' John said, clucking to Horse, who moved off slowly.

'It's a pretty steep path,' Lauren said, feeling more than a little anxious at the sudden warmth that seeped through her from John's body so close behind her. She shifted her weight nervously. 'Can this old horse manage it?'

John tucked an arm around Lauren. 'If you can, he can,' he replied. 'I trimmed his hoofs this morning. He won't stumble. Just tell me which way to go.'

'The path branches off the path that goes to the cabin where the Rodgers family is staying,' Lauren replied. 'The farthest west one.'

They found the path and started down, Lauren clutching the pommel of the saddle for dear life.

'I can tell you're not much of a rider,' John said, a note of amusement in his voice. 'We'll have to remedy that. Relax and lean back.' His arm tightened and he pulled her against him.

Lauren leaned back, but she could not relax. Between worry about Brian and John's overwhelming nearness she could scarcely breathe. The path twisted and turned, Horse negotiating it calmly, as if he knew that someone skilful was in control. At last they reached the point where the sound of rushing water tumbling over the rocks below could be heard. Mixed with that sound was the unmistakable high-pitched lilt of childrens' voices.

'I hear Brian,' Lauren said, relieved. 'He must have

come down here with the Rodgers family.' Moments later the children, accompanied by their father, appeared.

'Hi, Mommy! Hi, John,' Brian said, beaming. 'Can I go for a ride, too?'

Before Lauren could reply, the children's father spoke. 'Well, well. Good morning, Mrs Stanley,' he said. 'Out for a morning ride? It sure is a beautiful day. I'm going to have to get a fishing licence and try that stream for trout. How is it, do you know?'

'Very good,' Lauren replied.

'Oh, Dad,' one of the girls whined, 'I thought you were going to take us to see the dead volcano today.'

'I will, I will,' the man said patiently. 'I'll do some fishing this evening and early in the morning. The cabin is available, isn't it?' he questioned, looking hopefully at Lauren.

'Yes, it is,' she replied, then smiled at the little girl. 'Mount Lassen isn't a dead volcano,' she told her. 'It's only sleeping.' Then she turned her attention to Brian. 'Young man,' she said, 'I'd appreciate it if you'd let me know where you're going. I was worried about you.'

Brian looked sheepish. 'I was going to see John,' he said, 'but I looked in and he was gone, so I went back outside. I heard these guys starting to yell about wanting to do something, so I took them down to the creek.'

The children's father gave Lauren a knowing glance, and then patted Brian's head. 'I'm mighty glad you did take us there, Brian,' he said. 'I do love trout fishing. But next time, tell your mother first. I know how I'd worry if one of my kids disappeared in these woods.'

'I will,' Brian said soberly. Then he looked up at John and smiled hopefully. 'Can I have a ride back?' he asked.

John shook his head. 'I don't think so. Not since you went off without permission. Besides, I don't think your mother should have to walk back up, and Horse can't carry three people. Maybe tomororw morning, if you're extra good today, I'll take you for a ride. If it's all right with your mother.'

Brian's face fell, but he did not protest. 'Is it all right tomorrow?' he asked.

'We'll see,' Lauren replied. 'If you're extra good.'

At that, Brian smiled happily, and John wheeled Horse and started back up the hill after Lauren had assured the Rodgerses that breakfast would be served whenever they were ready, and no, the volcano was not about to wake up and erupt any time soon.

Brian's complete trust and adoration for John were so obvious that Lauren felt as if she were being torn in two directions at once. It was so good to see her son happy. John was so good with him. She often felt guilty that she did not want to contemplate marriage again. A boy needed a father. Maybe if she were somewhere where she might meet a suitable man it would be different, but not even for Brian could she marry Mel. Especially not for Brian. And John was certainly not the right man, either. Not that she didn't like him, too. It seemed impossible not to like him. But somebody had to plan for the future. She did not want to spend her life living from hand to mouth, from day to day, as John seemed perfectly happy to do. There was little enough security in a normal kind of life, as she knew only too well.

When they again reached Horse's little paddock, John dismounted and then helped Lauren down. He kept his hands lightly on her waist. 'Feel better now?' he asked.

Lauren nodded. 'I'm sorry that I . . .'

'I know,' John interrupted. 'I understand. You haven't know me long and there are a lot of unpleasant things that happen in the world. I've seen more than my share of them. But, believe me, I'd never do anything to hurt Brian, or anyone, if I could help it. I don't like to see people hurt, physically or otherwise.' He smiled ruefully. 'I've sometimes got into trouble from being too much that way.'

'I think, if I'd thought about it, I could have guessed that,' Lauren said. She could remember so vividly how John's eyes had mirrored her own pain when she'd told him her husband was dead. She also remembered that he had sounded pure Texas at that time. Now he did not sound that way at all. She cocked her head and gave John a critical look. 'Your drawl seems to have disappeared awfully fast,' she said. 'Which one is the real John Smith?'

John grinned. 'Why ma'am, I think we both are,' he drawled. 'Now y'all just mosey along and get that breakfast ready. I'm hungry enough to eat a couple of sides of Texas beef.'

'Y'all will have to settle for bacon and eggs and some of Isobel's special bran muffins and strawberry jam,' Lauren replied. She removed John's hands from her waist, but he caught her hands and held on to them. 'Stop that, John,' she said, pulling in a vain effort to free herself. 'Hurry up and get Horse put away. I think I'm going to need help in the dining-room.'

'Yes, ma'am,' John said. 'I'll be right there.' His eyes flicked over Lauren's face, his hands still holding hers tightly. Then he smiled and let them go, and turned to take Horse back to his stall.

He certainly was good at making sure things were done the way he wanted and when he wanted, Lauren thought crossly, rubbing her wrists as she walked back to the lodge. It still remained to be seen whether that included getting some of the repairs done around the lodge. After all, she hadn't hired him to exercise her horse or wait on tables!

Once the breakfast rush was out of the way, Lauren took John to see the combination storage shed and workshop that Paul had built behind the lodge.

'It's a pretty complete workshop,' John commented, looking around at the array of power tools. 'I should be able to fix almost anything with this equipment.'

'Paul did all of the building himself,' Lauren said. 'The lodge was in bad shape when we bought it, but he fixed it up and then built the cabins. We'd planned on another three cabins behind the lodge, and eventually on adding a wing to the lodge and expanding the dining-room. I don't expect that will ever happen now.' She shrugged and smiled wryly at John. 'I'd be happy just to have everything in good repair for a change. I think we'd better make a list of what needs to be done, don't you? Then we can check them off as you get them accomplished.'

John raised one eyebrow and studied Lauren thoughtfully. 'And when the list is finished, I go?' he asked softly.

Lauren swallowed, feeling a flush come to her cheeks. 'Something like that,' she said weakly, unable to meet John's eyes as she did so. How could he see through her so easily?

'Lauren,' John said, lifting her chin with his fingers until she was forced to look into his eyes, 'I don't think . . .' His voice trailed off, his expression tense. His eyes wandered from Lauren's down to her lips, and his own mouth tightened, as if he were trying to quell a strong desire to kiss her. Lauren held her breath, unable to move or speak. Then, suddenly, John looked up and past Lauren and dropped his hand to his side.

'I think your friend Mel is coming,' he said in a low voice. 'You'd better get your act together. You look like a woman who wants very much to be kissed.'

CHAPTER THREE

'I DO not!' Lauren denied, her flaming cheeks confirming that she lied. For, if she looked the way she felt, John was doubtless right. She pushed past him and opened a cupboard, rummaging frantically in her efforts to get herself under control. There must be something in here she wanted to find. The sign. It needed painting. She grasped a small can of paint as if it were a lifesaver. 'Here it is,' she said brightly, holding up the can. 'This is what we used to do the sign lettering before. I hope it's still all right.'

'Hello, Mr Cranston,' John's voice said behind her.

'Smith,' Mel said, nodding abruptly. 'What are you up to, Lauren?'

'Finding paint,' Lauren said, smiling at him in what she hoped was her usual manner. 'John's going to redo the sign tonight.'

Mel looked at her suspiciously. 'I thought you had a lot of more important stuff to fix than your sign lettering,' he said. 'Or can't Smith handle the harder work?'

'Of course he can!' A flash of anger almost made Lauren lose control of her temper. She clenched her jaw, trying to calm herself before she spoke. John quietly stepped into the void.

'Mrs Stanley was about to make a list for me,' he said.

Lauren shot him a grateful glance, and then smiled

at Mel. 'Can you remember some of the things I've been complaining about?' she asked. 'There are so many, I'm afraid I won't remember them all.'

'Well,' Mel said, obviously pleased at being consulted, 'there was a loose light fitting, some doors that didn't shut right, a bureau that needed refinishing on the top, some cabinets that don't stay closed . . .'

'The leak in the porch roof on the lodge and the rotten planks at the end of the porch, a cracked window-pane that needs replacing,' Lauren added, 'and most of the lodge windows need recaulking. We hired a high-school boy to help, and he didn't do it very well.' She poked around in the cabinet again. 'There's still some caulking compound in here. Why don't you start on that project, John? It has to be done while the weather's good. I'll make the list later.'

'Fine,' John said, nodding. He took a caulking gun from a hook on the wall, and then looked at Lauren, who was watching him, not knowing whether she ought to see if he knew how to do the job or not. 'You can go on about your work,' he said, with that amused little smile of his. 'I know how to do it.'

'I never doubted you did,' Lauren said defensively. 'I was trying to remember if there was anything else I should tell you. I guess there isn't.' She turned and followed Mel out of the door, feeling a tingling sensation between her shoulder-blades, as if she knew that John was watching her.

When they had gone a short distance, Mel said, 'I tracked down the place where Smith worked in Texas and called the people. Seems there's a new owner there.'

'You did?' Lauren stopped and frowned. 'That wasn't necessary! That's exactly what he told me. The people he worked for sold out and retired.'

'I thought it was necessary,' Mel replied. 'I don't want some derelict hanging around my favourite girl. But you don't need to look so upset. It seems they heard nothing but good things about your John Smith and were sorry he wouldn't stay on. Funny thing, though. There's a story among the ranch hands that John Smith isn't his real name. Kind of makes me wonder if he's hiding from something.' Seeing Lauren's dark scowl, he added in placating tones, 'Not necessarily anything criminal. Maybe just a tax collector.'

Lauren bit her lip. Remember, she told herself firmly, Mel is only trying to be helpful. 'That's ridiculous,' she said as casually as she could manage. 'I think everyone reacts that way to the name John Smith. I know I did. But, as he said, somebody has to have that name.'

Mel shrugged. 'Maybe. But I don't think you'd better get too used to having him around to help. Some day he'll just be moving on. That's the way fellows like him are. Meanwhile, I'd kind of like to know more about the guy. If you could get me a glass he's used, I could lift a set of fingerprints and see if there's anything on file about him.'

'I will not!' Lauren said vehemently, feeling her temper inching past simmer again. 'Mel Cranston, I want you to stop playing bloodhound. Go track down whoever stole Elvira Bloomer's lawnmower and leave me and John Smith alone! You found out that his last employer liked him. Let it go at that.'

'All right, all right,' Mel said, his round face unperturbed. 'I'm just naturally curious, that's all. It goes with my line of work. Well, I'd better be going. Don't work too hard, sweetheart.'

'I won't,' Lauren replied, squelching her desire to remind Mel for the thousandth time that she was not his sweetheart. With John Smith around, that would only add fuel to his unfounded jealousy. 'See you later,' was all that she said, as he got into his patrol car, and she breathed a sigh of relief when he had gone.

It was too bad, she thought as she went into the lodge, that Mel wasn't someone she could confide in. She was even more curious about John than Mel was, but the idea of sneaking his fingerprints was disgusting to her, almost like stealing something very personal from him would be. No, if she were ever to find out more about John, it would have to be because he trusted her enough to tell her, and it was questionable if he would. She had a strong feeling from what he had started to say before Mel had appeared that the fact that she was attracted to him disturbed him. He probably thought that her two lonely years without Paul was the cause, and felt sorry for her. Maybe he was afraid she was going to throw herself at him. Or it could be that he was going to warn her that he was only passing through, and if she got hurt it was her own stupid fault. Oh, why couldn't she react to him as if he were short, fat, ugly and mean? Because he was just the opposite, that was why!

'Well, what am I supposed to do, turn into a block of ice?' Lauren muttered to herself. She couldn't help it if she had a strong physical reaction to John Smith. Apparently she couldn't hide the fact from him, so she had best stay away from him as much as possible. If she worked inside and he worked outside, that shouldn't be too difficult.

But her plan had no sooner hatched than it was scuttled. Lauren was changing the bed in Room Three when there was a tap on the window. Lauren turned the stiff handle on the casement and opened it to John.

'You don't seem to know the value of oil,' he remarked with a mischievous twinkle, pointing to the casement handle. 'Try it some time.'

'I will,' Lauren replied crossly. 'Right in between peeling the potatoes and changing the beds. Did you want something?'

'I thought we could talk while we both work,' John replied, scraping away at the old caulking.

'What about?' Lauren asked, a premonitory twinge of anxiety making her tense.

'About what happened earlier,' John replied. 'I think maybe it's best if I only stay for a week. I should be able to get most of the things you mentioned done in that time.'

Only a week? Lauren felt as if her heart had suddenly plummeted into her stomach. 'I—I'm sorry to hear that,' she said hoarsely, stopping her work and turning to face the window. 'Is . . . is it my fault, or because of Mel's snooping around?'

'Neither,' John replied, shaking his head. 'I don't want any emotional entanglements, and I'm afraid there might be some here.'

'Oh.' Lauren turned back to the unmade bed, her eyes smarting with hot tears. Why should she feel like crying? What did she care if John didn't want any emotional entanglements? She didn't either! She beat the pillows fiercely into shape, then threw the spread on to the bed and jerked it straight with far more vigour than necessary.

'Lauren?' John said. 'I expected more of a response than that. Aren't you going to lecture me about maturity and responsibility and all of those good things?'

Lauren turned to face him, tears now streaming down her cheeks. 'Why should I?' she demanded. 'You're a coward, running from life, not living it. Keep on running. What do I care?' She turned and ran from the room, slamming the door behind her. A moment later, she opened the door again. 'The bureau in here is the one that needs refinishing,' she shouted. 'Some other irresponsible idiot spilled liquor all over it!'

With that, she ran down the hall and into her bathroom to splash cold water over her face. The last thing she wanted was for Brian to see that she had been crying. He had seen enough of that the first few months after Paul had died to last him a lifetime. Besides, she really didn't understand why she was crying. She'd known John Smith for a scant twenty-four hours. Why should she care so much if he only stayed a week?

For the rest of the afternoon, until dinnertime, Lauren successfully avoided seeing John Smith, although Brian ran happily back and forth between them, reporting on John's progress. By dinnertime she felt quite calm again. John appeared for dinner wearing a flannel shirt against the sudden coolness of the evening. The soft shirt made his broad shoulders and spare frame look warm and inviting. Lauren's calm disappeared and a tight ache invaded her throat. She could only trust herself to say a curt 'hello'. John was equally taciturn. They studiously avoided looking at each other. Isobel looked at them speculatively but said nothing. Brian was not so inhibited. As soon as he had figured out that something was amiss he spoke right up.

'Did you guys have a fight or something?' he demanded, coming to stand in front of Lauren, who was checking an order.

'Of course not, dear,' she replied. She hated to lie to Brian, but consoled herself with the thought that she and John had not really had a fight. All the yelling had been on her side. Out of the corner of her eye, she could see John looking at her, one eyebrow raised.

'I think your mother had a fight. I sort of stood and watched,' John said, a humorous quirk at the corner of his mouth.

Brian frowned up at Lauren. 'Are you mad at John?' he demanded.

'No!' Lauren said sharply. She glanced at John. 'Yes!' She hurriedly picked up the tray and went into the dining-room, plastering a pleasant smile on her face for the benefit of her guests. When she returned to the kitchen, John was just finishing putting another order together. When Lauren reached for the tray, he bent and whispered in her ear.

'I think that technically what we had was a lovers' quarrel,' he said.

'A . . .' Lauren swallowed the rest of the sentence and stared at John. 'I—can't imagine how you reached that conclusion,' she said. The sound of ice tinkling made her look down at the tray. It was shaking in her hands.

'Let me,' John said, actually grinning at her this time as he took the tray from her.

Lauren watched him go through the door, her mind in a whirl. First he said he was leaving in a week, now this! What on earth was going on?

'Are you trying to drive me crazy?' she demanded as soon as he returned.

'Not consciously,' he replied. 'Am I doing it?'

'Yes! First you . . .' Lauren looked at Brian's attentive little face and stopped. 'We'll discuss it later,' she said tightly.

'Good idea,' John agreed. 'A discussion was what I had in mind all along.'

When dinner was over and Brian tucked into bed, John suggested that Lauren come along while he got the sign and took it to his cabin to paint it.

'You're safe as long as my hands are busy,' John said as Lauren hesitated.

Lauren frowned. 'I don't think you're concerned about any emotional involvement,' she said coldly. 'I think all you're interested in is sex.'

'I think they go together,' John replied.

'Well, at least we agree on something,' Lauren said, following John towards the jeep without actually having agreed to do so. 'The sign's held up with padlocks. I've got the keys,' she said when John looked at her questioningly. When he held out his hand for the keys, she shook her head. 'I'll come along,' she said. 'I want to find out what you really meant by some of the things you said today.'

John silently opened the jeep's door for Lauren, then went around and got into the driver's seat. He was quiet, as he so often was, and Lauren wondered whether he was trying to prepare some answers to the questions she knew she would ask or was simply not thinking about anything at all. From the impassive set of his angular features, she could not tell.

'Wouldn't you be able to see better at the workshop?' she asked, as John lugged the heavy sign through his door.

'I've got a light,' John replied. He reached up and flooded the room with light from one bare bulb, hanging from a beam.

'When did you do that?' Lauren asked, amazed.

'Some time between being yelled at and dinner,' he replied, with a meaningful lift of one eyebrow and a quick glance at Lauren. 'Bringing in one wire was easy. It will take a bit longer to rewire this side of the cabin.'

Lauren gave him a sideways look. 'Longer than a week?' she asked.

'Considerably,' John replied. He propped the sign against a chair, pulled another chair over for Lauren to sit on, and then changed the subject. 'This is a beautiful sign,' he said, tracing the outline of the hand-carved raised letters. 'Did your husband do this?'

'No, a woodcarver from one of the logging camps,' Lauren answered. 'Why did you say you were going to leave in a week if you didn't mean it?'

'I meant it at the time,' John said, beginning to stir

the paint. 'I didn't realise . . .' He did not seem able to finish his sentence, rather deliberately directing all of his attention to adding some turpentine to the paint.

'Realise what?' Lauren asked. If John had some idea that she was falling in love with him, she had better set him straight right now. It was a long way from finding him very attractive to being in love.

'How much you wanted me to stay,' he answered, flicking a glance at her. 'You made that very plain.'

Lauren looked down and studied her hands, clenched in her lap. She couldn't really deny that. What John said was doubtless true. 'But what about your fear of emotional involvements?' she asked. 'I should think that only makes it worse for you.'

'I'm not afraid, Lauren,' John said, stopping his work and turning to look directly at her. 'I thought about it a lot this afternoon. I'm much more afraid of a world where there aren't any real emotions except greed and hatred and ambition . . . and revenge.'

He turned back to his work, and Lauren stared at him thoughtfully. That statement, she thought, must be a clue to his past. Greed, hatred and ambition were characteristics often ascribed to the wealthy. Sometimes cruel revenge, too. Was that the reason John seemed to come from somewhere different than his occupation would indicate? Could John have come from a background of wealth and ambition? Perhaps if she inched into the topic of his family, she might get some clues.

'You sound bitter,' she said. 'As if you've had intimate experience with those things.'

'I have,' John said shortly.

'Your family?' Lauren asked. She flinched at the

hard, cold look that John gave her.

'I don't want to discuss it,' he said in a voice as frigid as his expression.

'I—I'm sorry,' she said. 'I was only going to ask if you had any brothers or sisters, and what they were like if you did.'

John took a deep breath, appearing to get himself under control again. 'I shouldn't have snapped at you,' he said. 'Naturally, you're curious. Yes, I have a younger stepbrother and sister. They don't like me, and I'm not especially fond of them, either.'

'They don't like you?' Lauren could not imagine anyone really disliking John, not even a stepbrother and sister. 'I can't believe they really don't,' she said slowly. 'Just because you argue with people doesn't necessarily mean you don't care about them.'

'Lauren,' John said, stopping his work again and turning to face her, 'I'm sure you must have a nice, warm, affectionate family and it's hard for you to believe that there are people that aren't that way. But, believe me, my stepbrother, at least, would just as soon I was dead, and my stepsister doesn't give a damn one way or the other. Neither, as a matter of fact, does my stepmother. I'm not quite sure where my father stands. As a result, I have no contact at all with them any more.'

'Is it . . . because of the way you live?' Lauren asked, trying to understand this strange, horrid family. 'They don't think you're ambitious or greedy enough?'

John smiled wryly. 'Oh, I measured up quite well on their greedy and ambitious scale for a long time. No, it has nothing to do with that. Maybe some day

I'll tell you about it.' He came towards Lauren, bent, and pretended to dab paint on her nose. 'Enough about my dark and miserable past. It's your turn. Tell me about your family. I'm sure they're much nicer.'

Lauren rubbed her nose self-consciously. What little John had told her made her more curious than ever, but she could certainly understand why he was reluctant to talk about it. Maybe later, a little at a time, she could learn more. While John went back to his painting, she gave him a brief synopsis of her life.

'I think my family was pretty average,' she said. 'My parents were both schoolteachers in a little town in the Sacramento valley. I didn't have any brothers or sisters, so I was probably a little spoiled, but there wasn't enough money to spoil me very much. I went to college and got my teaching credentials. I met Paul the summer before I graduated, when I was working as a waitress at a resort near Mount Shasta. He was a management trainee there. After I graduated, we got married and I taught the first year and he was assistant manager then. We talked about having our own holiday lodge some day. Then, just after I found out I was expecting Brian, my parents were killed in a wreck when they were on vacation down in Baja California. I inherited their house, so we sold it and bought the run-down lodge and property here. Things were just getting going when Paul was killed. I've tried to keep things going, but I don't know how much longer I'll be able to. I may have to give up and go back to teaching.'

Lauren fell silent, brooding unhappily over that option, which she so hated to consider. She looked up to see John staring at her, his own expression profoundly sad. She raised her eyebrows questioningly.

'I don't like to think of you being so alone,' he said huskily. 'You don't have any other family to turn to to help out?'

'No.' Lauren shook her head. 'Unless you count my father's alcoholic brother, who's apt to show up here, looking for a handout.' She smiled wryly at John. 'I guess we're both alone when it comes to family ties.'

John swore softly and turned back to his work, but stood with his hand poised, motionless. 'I guess we are,' he said slowly. He put his paintbrush down and came to crouch in front of Lauren. He took her hands in his, looking for a long time at her small, pale hands engulfed in his large, deeply tanned and harshly callused hands. With his thumb, he stroked the finger which still bore her gold wedding ring. 'I should warn you,' he said, looking up and searching her face intently, 'that when I spoke of emotional entanglements before, I meant love and marriage. The whole thing. If I stay, I won't back off, and I won't let you, either. Not that I think you really want to.'

Lauren tried to pull her hands free. So he did think that she was falling in love with him! She jerked against the firm grip of John's hands, and frowned when he did not release hers. 'You're certainly presumptuous enough,' she said stiffly. 'Maybe you should just speak for yourself, John. The fact that I want you to stay doesn't mean . . . anything else. I need your help, that's all.'

'Come on, Lauren,' John said reprovingly. 'Be honest with yourself and with me. You didn't have that little fit this afternoon just because you wanted your windows caulked.'

Was he right? Was she falling in love with him? Lauren licked her lips nervously. She didn't want to think about loving him. It was too soon. Too frightening. 'I—I just don't like things all unsettled,' she said. 'First you said you'd stay, then you said you were leaving. It made me upset.'

'I know. I won't do that again. I'll be here.' John stood up, still holding Lauren's hands, and pulled her to her feet, his eyes never leaving hers.

Lauren stared into his vividly blue eyes, her heart racing thunderously. Was John going to kiss her? The very thought of it made her dizzy. When his arms closed around her, she trembled. At first she stood rigid. This wasn't right. It was the first time since Paul died that a man who aroused her physically had held her in his arms. She felt guilty. At the same time, the longing for the feeling of security that being enclosed, comforted and protected again by masculine arms provided was so strong that she felt torn almost in two. She burst into tears and buried her face in her hands.

John's arm tightened around her, and Lauren could feel his cheek brushing against her hair, his lips soft against her ear. After a moment he began to sing, in a deep, warm voice, the old folk song: ' "Hush little baby, don't you cry, Daddy's going to sing you a lullabye; hush little darlin', don't say a word, Daddy's going to buy you a mockingbird; and if that mockingbird don't sing, Daddy's goin' to buy you a diamond ring; and if that diamond rings turns brass, Daddy's goin' to buy you a looking-glass . . ." '

Gradually, as he sang, Lauren's tears subsided. Her

arms stole around John. She leaned against him and closed her eyes, aware only of a warm strength seeming to enter her body from his, the regular rhythm of his heart, and the gentle touch of his hands.

'Feel better now?' John asked softly.

Lauren raised her head and nodded. His face was so close to hers. She had never noticed that half-moon shaped scar beneath his chin, nor the way little lines tilted away from the corners of his mouth, as if waiting for him to smile.

'You have a beautiful voice,' she said.

'I never used to sing before I spent time alone, out under the stars,' he said. 'When I tried it, I liked the way it made me feel. Sort of comfortable with the world.'

'It made me feel better,' Lauren said. 'I guess that's one of those things we do for children, and then forget that adults might like it too. Thank you, John.'

John looked embarrassed. 'I'm glad it helped. My horse seemed to like it,' he said, with a self-deprecating smile. He caught her face with his hand and traced her lips with his thumb. All the while, he looked into her eyes, soberly, as if were trying very hard to see what she was thinking so that he might not frighten her away again. 'I was going to kiss you,' he said, 'but I don't want to frighten you too much. Perhaps we would talk about the weather instead.'

'About the weather?' Lauren said hoarsely, her eyes following the movement of John's lips as he spoke, as if they had a will of their own. His lips looked so soft, so warm and inviting.

'Yes, about the weather. How early does it snow up here?' he asked, bending his head towards her just a little.

'Sometimes . . . in October,' she answered, trying to focus on John's blue eyes with their heavy fringe of dark lashes. They were getting so much closer. Was he thinking about kissing her now, after all? 'But it usually doesn't stay long,' she breathed, her heart beginning to skip erratically. 'The heavy snows are higher in the mountains.'

'Do you like to ski?' he asked.

'Oh, yes. Do you?' Lauren held her breath, watching John's mouth come ever closer to her own. He was going to kiss her. She shouldn't let him. But she wanted him to.

'I love to,' he replied. He brushed his lips against Lauren's, sending a shiver of excitement through her. For a moment he paused, his eyes flicking around her face, seemingly unsure of whether to kiss her more firmly or not.

Please kiss me, John, she thought. I have to know how it feels. As if he had heard her, or was having the same thoughts, he gave a deep groan and covered her mouth with his.

At first, Lauren felt as if all of her senses were on hold. She felt suspended, waiting, like a child who has lighted a fuse on a firecracker. Then, suddenly, the explosion came, and a flood of excitement rushed through her like a shockwave. It seemed as if the room were swaying and swinging crazily around her. Her arms closed around John's back, clinging to him for support. When John's tongue tickled slowly along her lips, she opened her mouth to him, teasing back, and then plunging her tongue into his mouth to slide along the soft, smooth inner surface of his lips, and taste the sweet deliciousness of his essence. John's hands moved eagerly over her body, pausing to press her firmly against him, then smoothing her to him as if welding her there. For a long time they clung together, bodies straining to be close, their lips communicating messages of longing and desire back and forth like a heady wine being poured from one bottle to another. It felt, Lauren thought wonderingly, as if she had come in from a long time in a world of cold and darkness, to one of warmth and dazzling brightness. At last John loosened his grip and slowly raised his head. Etched deeply in the translucent blue of his eyes was a look of such triumphant happiness that Lauren could only stare back at him, still feeling breathless and a little dizzy.

'I'd like to think of something profound to say right now,' he said huskily, 'but for the life of me I can't think of anything even intelligent.'

'Neither can I,' Lauren replied. She felt elated and terrified at the same time. Elated because she had felt an excitement that she had thought she might never feel again. Terrified because, if that excitement meant what John thought it did, it was at the wrong time, in the wrong place, and with the wrong man!

CHAPTER FOUR

LAUREN backed away from John. 'Maybe there isn't anything profound to say,' she suggested. 'After all, there's nothing terribly significant about a physical reaction between a man and a woman. I—I think I'll just leave you to your sign-painting now.' She didn't care what John thought about how disturbed she was by his kiss. She needed to get away from this room, in which his dominating presence seemed to permeate every inch of the space.

John raised one eyebrow and looked amused, but made no reply. He picked up his paintbrush again. 'Sit down for a minute,' he said. 'I wanted to ask you about the financial problems you have. You said the Redferns had made you an offer?'

'Yes,' Lauren replied, reluctantly perching on the edge of her chair. 'But that was a long time ago. Right after the forest fire. And right after . . . well, I don't know if you remember, but one of their own sons disappeared at about that time. I could never understand . . . they didn't even offer me any condolences or anything. Their other son, Kevin, showed up here and acted as if it was business as usual. He was really nasty when I turned him down, as if I owed it to them to take their measly offer. Well, I wouldn't, and I've managed to almost keep up the payments. The bank gave me an extension on part of the payment last year, but I don't know if they'll do it again. If I have to give up the lodge . . .' Lauren stopped, the thought making her miserable.

John was silent for so long, his expression so grim, that Lauren wondered if perhaps hearing about her financial situation had made him have second thoughts about staying. 'In case you were looking for a rich wife,' she said coolly, 'I'm not it.'

At that John exploded. 'For pete's sake, Lauren, do you take me for an idiot?' He spoke so loudly that Lauren flinched visibly. Then he smiled wryly. 'Sorry. I was thinking about the—er—tactlessness of the Redferns just now. I also think I should take a look at your books tomorrow. Maybe there's something we can do to stave off disaster.'

A look at her books? We? Did John Smith think that one kiss entitled him to take over her entire life? 'Don't tell me you're an accountant, too,' Lauren snapped, getting to her feet, 'because I won't believe it. If you were, you'd have a decent job instead of hitch-hiking around the country dressed like a cowboy and pretending to have a Texas drawl. I'm beginning to wonder if I can believe anything you've told me.'

'Then I guess you'll have to add this to the list of things you don't believe,' John said calmly. 'I'm not an accountant, but I do have a Master's degree in business administration, and a number of years' experience. Others would be willing to pay thousands of dollars for my consulting services, if I were inclined to offer them. Which I am not.'

Lauren sank slowly back down in her chair. Either John was totally crazy, or he was the strangest, most fascinating man she had ever encountered. 'Why . . . why aren't you?' she asked.

'Because,' John replied, bending close to his work and carefully tracing a corner of a letter, 'I hated it. I'm sure you've heard high-stakes business described as being a rat race. That's exactly the way it felt. Hundreds of rodents churning through a maze, each one trying to claw his way through the opening ahead of the others.' He gave Lauren a serious look. 'I'd do almost anything for you, Lauren,' he said, 'but I wouldn't go back to that, no matter what.'

There he goes again, Lauren thought, shaking her head in bemusement and watching as he went back to his painting. He was assuming his role in her life as if it were a foregone conclusion, and at the same time warning her that certain options were not available when it came to getting money. That could either mean that the money was not as readily available as he would like her to think, or that he really had found it an unbearable existence. Should she let him look at her account books? There was nothing secret there. And if he could help . . .

It was not too hard to imagine, she thought, as she watched his deft, precise movements restore the faded lettering to its original deep red colour, that he had at one time been a successful businessman. The bones of his wrists were small, his fingers long and straight. His shoulders were wide and square, his waist slender. He would look tremendously elegant in evening clothes. For a moment she let herself picture him that way, then shook her head. She was never likely to see him in them.

'There,' he said at last, standing up and wiping his hands with a rag. 'Is that satisfactory?'

'Very,' Lauren replied. 'It looks two hundred per

cent better. Now people who see it won't think the inn-keeper is a lazy person who most likely has a poorly kept lodge. I should have thought of that angle before, shouldn't I? I guess I'm not a very good businesswoman.'

John shrugged as he cleaned his paintbrush. 'There are only so many hours in the day to do things. I think you've done remarkably well at keeping things up.' He bent and flicked a speck of paint away from the edge of a letter. 'It should be dry by morning. I'll hang it back up then.'

Lauren stood up again. 'Well, I guess I'd better go back to the lodge. I'll leave the jeep here so you can take the sign back. You—you can look over the books after breakfast, if you want.'

'Even though I may barely know how to add and subtract?' John teased. 'Wait a minute, and I'll walk you back.' He finished cleaning his brush, scrubbed his hands meticulously, then took Lauren's arm and walked silently beside her down the soft, pine-needle-covered path. When they stopped at the steps of the lodge, Lauren looked up at him.

'You really do have an MBA, don't you?' she said.

'Mm-hm,' John nodded. 'I really do.'

Lauren shook her head and sighed. 'I don't think I understand you very well,' she said.

John smiled. 'Sometimes I don't understand myself,' he said. He bent and gave Lauren a swift kiss on the cheek. 'If Brian wants to go riding with me in the morning, send him over as soon as he's up. That is, if he was good enough today to deserve it. As far as I could tell, he was.'

'He was almost too good,' Lauren said. 'I could tell

how hard he was trying.'

'Motivation does wonders,' John said with a grin. 'Goodnight, angel.'

'Goodnight, John,' Lauren replied.

She watched until he was out of sight, then went up the steps and into the lodge. She looked in at Brian, sleeping soundly clutching his beloved teddy bear, Frank curled up on the rug beside his bed, his constant protector. The ache started in her heart again. They had both taken to John so quickly. John would be so easy to love. If the lodge couldn't be turned into a paying proposition, what would be so wrong with having a schoolteacher for a mother and a handyman for a father? Nothing, really, except that it would mean giving up the dream that she and Paul had shared of a place for families and young couples without a great deal of money to come and enjoy the beautiful mountains and streams. It would be like cutting Paul out of her life forever and giving her heart to another man who some day might not be there. She wasn't ready to do that. She wasn't sure she would ever be.

Lauren set her alarm for six a.m. as usual, but was awakened before it went off by the uncomfortable feeling that someone was in the room, watching her. She opened one eye. Brian was standing beside her bed, already fully dressed.

'Good heavens,' she said, raising her head and looking at her clock. 'It's only five-thirty. What are you doing up?'

'I'm going riding with John!' Brian said, his excitement obvious. 'Don't you remember?'

'Oh, *yes*,' Lauren groaned. 'I don't know if he's ready yet, but go ahead and wake him up, too. He deserves it. It was his idea.' She squinted at Brian's small form. 'Better wear your jacket. It's chilly this early.'

'OK,' Brian said, racing into his room. He was back in seconds, pulling on his jacket as he ran. 'Can I go now?'

'Go ahead,' Lauren said. She smiled wryly as Brian tore out of the door. He had no reservations about his relationship with John. It would be nice to be four years old, and not be able to foresee the problems that adults had to face.

It was almost time for breakfast, and Lauren was growing anxious, when Brian reappeared. 'We rode all around on the logging roads, and we talked to some of the guys who were cutting down trees,' he reported excitedly. 'John says I can come with him again some time soon, and he's going to teach me to ride by myself. Can we get another horse, Mommy?'

'Not any time soon,' Lauren replied. When John appeared in the kitchen a few minutes later she frowned at him. 'Now you've got Brian wanting another horse,' she said. 'As if I didn't have enough problems already.'

'Let's cross that bridge when we come to it,' John suggested in his usual unruffled manner. 'He has to learn to ride first.'

'He'd better be a slow learner,' Lauren said crossly. 'We can't afford . . .' She stopped as the kitchen door swung open. 'Oh, hello, Mel,' she said, as the young officer came through the door. 'You're here bright and early. Would you like some coffee?'

'Don't mind if I do,' Mel replied, giving Lauren a smile and a curt nod to John. He looked down at Brian, who was hopping up and down in front of him. 'What's got you all wound up, young fellow?' he asked.

Brian, still so excited that he was unusually talkative in front of Mel, poured out the story of his morning's adventure. 'Maybe some time we'll even get another horse so I can really go riding with John,' he concluded.

Mel did not share Brian's enthusiasm. He glared at John. 'Looks as if you're planning on hanging around for quite a while,' he said coldly.

'That's right,' John replied evenly, although Lauren could see a flash of anger cross his face.

'I don't think that's such a good idea,' Mel said, his eyes narrowing into angry slits. 'You'd better be out of here before the snow flies. It gets pretty cold, walking down the highway after that.'

John looked down at Mel from beneath his long lashes, his head still erect. Lauren thought that she had never seen a look of such icy contempt. 'Thank you for your concern, Cranston,' he said quietly. 'I'll manage my own life. You manage yours.'

'Why, you . . .' Mel started to get up, his face red with rage.

'Sit down, Mel,' Lauren said, immediately moving in front of him. 'John, would you please see if anyone in the dining-room needs more coffee?'

'Of course,' John replied, and quickly went out through the door.

'Needs to hide behind a woman's skirts, does he?' Mel sneered. 'Bums like him usually do.'

Lauren was already so angry that she could scarcely contain herself, but she was not going to tell Mel what she thought in front of Brian, who was staring at Mel with undisguised hatred. 'Come outside with me a minute, Mel,' she said, heading for the back door of the kitchen. 'We need to talk. Alone.'

'You bet we do,' Mel agreed, following her. As soon as he was outside he launched into a tirade without giving Lauren a chance to speak. 'What in the devil's going on in your head, letting that guy take Brian all over the place on horseback? He's only been here a couple of days. For all you know, he might be some kind of a pervert. What's he doing here, anyway? You found that out yet? Why does he want to go snooping around the timber crews? He's not no business with them. Nothing legal, anyway.'

'What on earth are you talking about?' Lauren demanded.

'Controlled substances,' Mel said portentously. 'Someone's been furnishing them to some of the guys up in the woods. I'll bet anything it's your friend John Smith, or some cohorts of his. People don't show up from out of nowhere and then hang around a place for no reason. Not for just room and board.'

'I—I never thought of that,' Lauren said lamely. 'But all he had with him was his pack. He didn't have room for something like that.'

'Doesn't take much room,' Mel said. 'Or he could have some stuff stashed in the woods. Sounded from what Brian said as if he knew his way around them pretty well.'

Lauren felt sick. Could Mel be right? Had she been completely taken in by John's easy charm? She remembered that he had seemed especially interested in whether Stoney Creek Lodge was near the place where she had had her flat tyre.

'I'll talk to Brian,' she said almost inaudibly. 'Maybe he saw something.'

Mel nodded. 'Good idea. I'll come back tonight and see if you found out anything. And don't let that guy pull any more wool over your eyes. You're just too trusting. If Brian saw anything suspicious, don't say anything to Smith. I'll get rid of him for you. I don't want you getting him riled up. He might be dangerous.'

'I'll be careful,' Lauren said. Very careful. A terrible chill went through her. She might have been entrusting Brian to a criminal of the worst kind!

Lauren had no chance to talk to Brian during the time breakfast was being served. She tried to maintain a normal demeanour, but she could see John looking at her curiously and knew that she was not succeeding very well.

All the while, doubts kept piling in on her. John Smith might have other names. Many others. Aliases. Criminals often did. Maybe the reason he was no longer a successful businessman was that he had found something more exciting, and profitable, to do. His poor clothing might be only a disguise, discarded when he took his ill-gotten gains to some fancy resort in another country. No wonder he looked as if he were used to associating with the wealthy! No wonder his family wanted nothing to do with him!

As soon as breakfast was over, she took John to her apartment and got her account books out of her desk. 'Here,' she said, handing them to him. 'Do your worst. Or better yet, figure out how to turn minuses into pluses. I'll be back in a few minutes. I have to have a talk with Brian.'

'Hurry back,' John said drily. 'I think we need to have a talk, too. Mel Cranston put some kind of a bee in your bonnet, didn't he?'

'Why, no,' Lauren said innocently. 'He was just his usual obnoxious self.' She turned and hurried out the door, afraid that she would not be able to look sweetly innocent for long under John's knowing surveillance.

Lauren took Brian out into the yard, where she knew no one could overhear them, and crouched down in front of him.

'I've got to ask you something very important,' she told him. 'When you and John were out riding this morning and stopped to talk to the lumberjacks, did you see him give anything to any of them?'

Brian frowned. 'No. Why, Mommy? Did he do something bad?'

'I don't know,' Lauren answered. 'That's why I'm trying to find out. Did he get off Horse at all?'

'Sure. When he was talking to some of those guys. I got to stay on Horse all by myself.'

'Well, think hard now, love. Could you see what he was doing all the time he was off Horse?' Lauren asked.

Brian scrunched his eyes almost shut. 'I don't think so,' he answered finally. 'But I wasn't always looking. I was watching a man climb up a tree. What's wrong, Mommy? Is John going to have to go away like Mel said?' His lip began to quiver.

'I hope not,' Lauren replied, ruffling his hair. 'Now, don't cry. There's nothing to cry about. And for goodness' sake, don't tell John what I've been asking you. It's a secret. That's very, very important. OK?'

'OK,' Brian agreed, his voice quavering.

Lauren sighed and stood up. She had been afraid that Brian would have nothing to report. If John were involved in something illegal, he was far too clever to let Brian see it. Now she had to go and face John, and see if she could be even more clever than he was, for a change. He had guessed that Mel had made her suspicious of something, and was probably several jumps ahead of her already. If she told him what Mel had said, he would doubtless pooh-pooh Mel's accusations as ridiculous. But Mel had told her not to say anything. John might be dangerous. She couldn't really believe that, but still, it would be foolish to find out too late that Mel was right. What should she do? She shook her head. Nothing brilliant came readily to mind. She might as well go and see what John said. Unless she was mistaken, John would lead the discussion, not shrink from it. He was not that way. The question was, did that mean he was honest, or only very devious?

'All right, out with it,' John said, as soon as Lauren entered her apartment, confirming her guess that he would not try to avoid the problem. 'Sit down and tell me what Mel said to you that's got you so upset. He seems to have convinced you that there's something about me to cause you concern. What is it?'

'It—it's not very nice,' Lauren said hesitantly. Now that she was face to face with John, her desire to confront him with Mel's accusations was rapidly evaporating. John could never do such a thing as

Mel had suggested. Could he?

'I'd guessed that much,' John said with an amused smile. 'Has he diagnosed me as some kind of psychopathic killer? There are several unsolved murders in Texas, not far from where I was. He could easily have found out about them.'

'There are?' Lauren said hoarsely.

John nodded. 'Six, to be exact. Of course, the man they're looking for is about a foot shorter than I am, and fifty pounds heavier, but I suppose Mel wouldn't notice that part.'

'He . . . he didn't mention any murders,' Lauren said.

'Maybe he'll pick up on that next,' John said with a sigh. 'What, then?' When Lauren did not answer immediately, he went on, 'Look, Lauren, Mel doesn't want me here. And I'm afraid it's not only because of you, although exactly what his other reason is, I'm not sure just yet. Maybe he sincerely thinks that I represent a potential one-man crime wave. The most obvious thing that he might suspect is that I'm a drug pusher. Is that it?'

'Y-yes,' Lauren answered, chilled by the way John had zeroed in on Mel's suspicions. 'How did you know?'

'Elementary, my dear,' John said with a smile. 'My keen powers of observation and my sense of smell told me this morning that there's some in the neighbourhood. Here I am, a lonesome stranger, and, from Mel's point of view, an undesireable character. It's an easy conclusion for him to jump to. Wrong, but easy. Did he have any real reasons to back up his accusations?'

'Well,' Lauren said reluctantly, 'he said that the fact that you want to stay here indefinitely, even though you're only getting room and board, doesn't exactly make sense any other way.'

'And you bought that?' John asked incredulously.

Lauren felt as if she were actually shrinking beneath John's intense stare. 'It—it sounded reasonable,' she stammered.

John leaned forward, angry sparks seeming to fly from the depths of his eyes. 'Are you saying that you think I'd deliberately lie about how I feel about you?' he demanded. 'Are you?'

'I—I don't know,' Lauren said hoarsely, now feeling utterly miserable. 'I don't know how you feel about me. You said things about what might happen, but you . . .' She choked to a halt, watching apprehensively as John got up and came towards her.

'Get up,' he commanded, stopping in front of her. When Lauren did not move, he reached down, took hold of her hand, and pulled her to her feet. He put his hands on her shoulders. 'Look at me,' he said, his voice dangerously soft. 'Look into my eyes. Do not, at any time, look anywhere else. And listen!' His last words came out as a loud roar. Then he dropped his voice again and went on. 'I am not a drug pusher. I am probably one of the few people my age who has never even *tried* a controlled substance. I would rather slit my own throat than sell anyone else any of that murderous stuff. I would rather do that than deceive you about how I feel. I didn't want to tell you exactly, because I thought it would be premature and put pressure on you to reciprocate, but I'm telling you right now. I love you, Lauren.' He gave her shoulders a little shake. 'I *love* you!' he repeated more loudly. 'Do you understand? I don't know how it happened so fast. I certainly didn't plan or expect it. But when I saw you out on the highway I knew you were the woman I'd always dreamed of finding to spend my life with. And somehow, in spite of everything, I am going to see that that dream comes true. But while I'm being truthful, I am going to confess to one thing. Mel is right that there is another reason I'm here. It was the reason I came to this area in the first place, but it has *nothing* to do with the reason that I'm so determined to stay with you, and no relationship at all to Mel's crazy ideas. I'll tell you about it as soon as I can. In the meantime, please, please say nothing to your friend Mel. That would only make a difficult job more difficult.' His mouth twisted into a wry grimace. 'There's not much else I can say on my own behalf. I know it's my word against an old friend's, but if there's anything you want to ask I'll try to answer you as completely as I can.'

Lauren bit her lip and shook her head. Her head was spinning from trying to understand what it might mean that John had wanted to be here, her emotions in a tangle at his declaration of love. 'Now I'm more confused than ever,' she complained. 'I don't know what to believe. Are you some kind of special agent?'

'Not exactly,' John said, 'but that's close enough. Just remember that I love you and forget the rest.' He pulled Lauren close and held her tightly against him, his cheek resting on her hair. 'You're still tied up in knots,' he said, massaging her shoulders with one hand.

'I know.' She looked up at John. He smiled, and she

felt her heart beat faster. 'I do so want to believe you,' she whispered. 'But I keep wondering if maybe you're just very clever and I'm very stupid. Mel keeps telling me that I am.'

John frowned and shook his head. 'Don't you believe him. You're not stupid at all. After all, you haven't been stupid enough to want to marry him, have you? Try to trust your own instincts a little more. And Brian's. You can sometimes fool children for a little while, but they usually figure out if someone isn't what they appear to be. No one can keep up an act all of the time.'

'I suppose that's true,' Lauren said slowly. 'Oh, dear. I—I had to ask Brian if he'd seen anything suspicious this morning when you were out riding, and now he's terribly worried.' Her eyes widened as John swore violently.

'Sorry,' he said quickly. 'I just don't want that meddling so and so causing Brian any grief. I wish you hadn't seen fit to bring Brian into this, but since you did I think that means you're going to have to choose sides, for his sake. Well, Lauren, which is it? Do you believe me or Mel?'

Lauren stared at John, trying to find the answer in her heart as well as her mind. Paul had thought the world of Mel, but ever since Paul died she had had a strangely negative feeling whenever Mel was near. She had thought it was only because he wanted more than friendship from her. But was that the only reason? Brian had been only a toddler when Paul was killed, but he had never taken to Mel, even though Mel had tried hard to make up to him. And Frank! He had hated Mel outright ever since he was a puppy.

None of those things proved anything, of course, but it did seem that she should give John the benefit of the doubt. She took a deep breath and gave John a little smile.

'I guess I'll go with you,' she said. 'You might be able to fool me and Brian, but I don't think you could fool Frank.'

For a moment, John said nothing. Then his lips twitched and he burst into laughter. 'Saved by a dog,' he said. 'Good old Frank.' His face grew serious again. 'Let's get Brian straightened out, and then get down to some serious business. I'm finding your accounting as hard to decipher as Egyptian hieroglyphics.'

CHAPTER FIVE

IT WAS several hours, and a great many muttered expletives, later that John finally announced that he knew exactly where Lauren stood financially. 'Lord only knows how you've muddled along as well as you have,' he said, shaking his head in despair. 'Didn't you learn anything about bookkeeping in college?'

'I taught third grade, not bookkeeping,' Lauren said sharply, offended by John's criticism. 'Your only problem was that you didn't understand my system.'

'System?' John said sarcastically, one eyebrow cocked. 'Only you, and possibly the Internal Revenue Service, would call this a system. Come over here and sit down and let me show you what I've done, and what you need to do from now on.'

'You certainly are bossy enough,' Lauren grumbled as she pulled a chair over next to John's. She peered at the papers he pushed in front of her. 'That looks sort of like the way Paul used to do it,' she said, 'but I didn't understand how it worked.'

John sighed. 'He should have shown you exactly how it worked so you wouldn't have been so confused when you had to do it yourself. Now, first of all . . .'

Lauren watched and listened intently, surprised that with John's clear explanations the mysteries of double-entry bookkeeping soon vanished. 'I wish I'd asked Paul to explain all that before,' she said with a grimace. 'It just never occurred to me that I'd need to know it.'

'That happens to a lot of women,' John replied. 'Some day we'll get a computer, but in the meantime I want you to keep this up to date.' He gave Lauren a direct, severe look. 'And that means every single day.'

'Yes, sir,' Lauren replied, no longer feeling that John was merely bossy. He really did know what he was talking about, and had doubtless given her some extremely valuable lessons. 'I certainly will.'

'Good. Now, if you can direct me to something that will tell me exactly what your mortgage payment is, and when it is due, we can soon tell if there's any hope of making it or not.'

'I'm not sure I want to know,' Lauren said sourly. She rummaged in her desk and pulled out a long envelope. 'Here. This tells all.'

John bent his dark head over his work again, his fingers flying, first over Lauren's little calculator, then over a page of figures that he jotted down in a bold, precise hand. He seemed unaware of Lauren, watching him anxiously. Now and then he paused to stare into space, then nodded and made more calculations. At last he stopped and looked up at Lauren.

'That bad?' Lauren asked, her heart sinking at his grim expression.

'Bad, but not impossible,' John replied. 'Just follow these figures.' He stabbed at the paper with his finger. 'As you can see, if you could keep two of the three cabins rented at all times, and nine of the ten lodge-rooms, it could be done if you raised your rates by just five dollars per day or twenty per week. That would mean you'd have to have the third cabin available for overlap, which I could have done in about a week.'

'But that *is* impossible!' Lauren cried. 'There have never been that many people here consistently. And after Labor Day . . .'

'Whoa!' John commanded. 'Are you going to sit there and tell me it can't be done, or do you want to try?'

At that moment, Lauren could well believe that John could earn large fees as a consultant. The intense sparkle in his eyes and the dynamic way he took command were too powerful to ignore. 'I want to try,' she replied quickly. 'But what do I do? What's going to make all of those people appear? Magic?'

'I think the most obvious thing is advertising,' John replied. 'I don't see anything in here . . .' he pointed to Lauren's account book, 'to indicate you've done anything more than have some pamphlets printed a couple of years ago.'

Lauren sighed. 'I've thought about it, but I never could decide where to advertise or how much, and I'm not very good at phrasing such things. Do you think I can afford it now? Won't that just eat up the profit we need to make?'

'You can't afford not to,' John said firmly, 'and right here,' he pointed to a figure, 'I've factored in a suitable amount in my calculations. A small ad that appears regularly in all of the major newspapers from the Oregon border to San Francisco would pay big dividends. There are publications that cater to retired people. They're a likely source of customers. If service stations in nearby towns would let you put up posters or leave a supply of pamphlets, that would help. Let the big resorts know you're available in case of overflow. Get the lodge listed in catalogues of resorts and motels.' He paused and looked up at Lauren, who was staring at him, speechless. 'Well?'

She smiled and shook her head. 'I was just thinking that when you listed the things you could do that day when I picked up a lonesome-looking hitch-hiker, you forgot a few.'

John lifted one eyebrow, his mouth twisted into a half-smile. 'Lady, as the old saying goes, "you ain't seen nothin' yet". Now, let's figure out what we want to say, and where we want to say it.'

'All right,' Lauren agreed. She frowned thoughtfully. 'How long do you think it will take to see some results?'

'A week or two,' John answered. 'I only wish this were June instead of almost the first of August. We'll have to concentrate on the autumn vacation periods and perhaps some weekend packages for people who live nearby. And it will be a good idea to make retired people a real target, since they aren't tied down to regular jobs and children's school terms.'

'Why didn't you show up sooner?' Lauren grumbled. 'Even if the advertising does get results, if may not be in time to stop the bank.'

'Don't be negative. It might give you enough ammunition to convince them to back off for a while,' John said firmly.

'Mel's going to wonder how I happened to get so smart all of a sudden,' Lauren said, with a sideways glance at John. 'I don't suppose I ought to tell him you helped.'

'I doubt he'd think it was so smart,' John said drily, 'since you say he wants you to sell out to the Redferns.

He'd think it was just another of my plots to subvert his interests. Why don't you just tell him that you read it somewhere, and desperation motivated you.' He tapped impatiently on the table with his pencil. 'Time's a-wasting. Find some blank paper, will you? And let's start being creative.'

'I think I can see how you got to be a leader in the rat race,' Lauren commented, as she found her supply of paper and handed it to John.

John only grinned. In a short time he had come up with a clever advertisement that said a great deal in a few words. He also drew a simple poster to have printed, with a charming likeness of the lodge in the background.

'Everyone will know I didn't do that,' Lauren said. 'I can't draw at all.'

'You can give me credit for the picture,' John said. 'That's the kind of thing Mel would expect a bum like me to be able to do.' He stood up from the table where he had been working and stretched. 'It's getting late. I'd better get cleaned up for dinner. We'll get things rolling first thing in the morning.'

'And then wait for the phone to start ringing off the hook?' Lauren asked with a wry little smile, still not convinced that anything would come of their work.

'Exactly,' John said, taking her hand in his. He carried her hand to his lips, and then held it against his cheek. 'Don't look so glum, angel,' he said. 'You'll be surprised at what will happen. I promise you.' He kissed her palm again, stared at her searchingly, then shook his head and sighed. 'How I wish I could wave a magic wand and make everything perfect for you,' he said.

'You've already done a lot,' Lauren said, holding tightly to his hand. 'Thank you.'

'Don't thank me yet,' John replied. He bent suddenly and kissed Lauren's lips. 'See you at dinner.'

After John had left, Lauren sat down in the chair where he had been working and stared at his neat columns of figures. If they were right, and as far as she could tell they were, there might yet be some hope for Stoney Creek Lodge, if his advertising ideas paid off as well as he hoped they would. She was trusting her whole future, financial as well as emotional, to him. And, only this morning, she had been wondering if she could trust him at all! No wonder her head was aching. It had been a traumatic day, and it wasn't over yet. There was dinner to supervise, supplies to inventory, and a dozen other little details to see to before bedtime. Sometimes, she thought wryly, it didn't make sense for her to want so desperately to keep the lodge. How simple it would seem to keep house for only one family, after going through this!

As Lauren had suspected he would, Mel appeared again at dinnertime. It never seemed to occur to him, she thought bitterly, that it cost her just as much to feed him as it did any of the paying guests. She also noticed that he finished his dinner and dessert before he came into the kitchen and motioned surreptitiously for her to follow him into the pantry.

'Did Brian see anything?' he asked, his eyes glittering hopefully. 'I noticed you and Smith didn't seem to be talking much tonight.'

'We've been busy, and I'm tired,' Lauren replied. 'No, Brian didn't see anything suspicious at all.'

Mel made an unpleasant, snorting sound. 'I was

afraid of that. Little whippersnapper would probably lie to protect his friend.'

Lauren felt the ache in her head begin to throb so violently that it felt as if the top of her head would burst open. Brian? A liar. For the first time in her life, she knew what it meant to be so angry that she saw red. 'How dare you call my son a liar?' she yelled, completely forgetting for the moment that she could probably be heard in the dining-room.

'Well, sometimes boys . . .' Mel stopped, his eyes growing wide as Lauren grabbed a large bottle of ketchup from the pantry shelf and brandished it in front of her.

'Get out of here, Mel!' she said in an only slightly more moderate tone of voice.

'Now, sweetheart, I just meant . . .' Mel began.

'Don't you call me sweetheart!' Lauren shrieked, raising the ketchup bottle over her head. 'Get out of here right now!'

'Just take it easy,' Mel said, raising his hands protectively in front of himself. 'Take it easy, Lauren.' He began to back towards the door, stumbling as he backed into John, who had come hurrying to see what the commotion was about.

John quickly sized up the situation and pushed past Mel. He took the bottle from Lauren's hand and put his arm around her. 'Calm down, Lauren,' he said. 'What's the trouble?'

'He called Brian a liar,' she replied, her voice still trembling with anger. 'He's not interested in the truth. He just wants to make trouble for you.'

'Oh, so you told him, did you?' Mel spat out the words in disgusted tones. 'Boy, Smith, you sure do have a way with the ladies, don't you? How many hundreds more have you played for suckers all over the country?'

'I'll leave that to your fertile imagination, Cranston,' John replied, his voice calm but razor-sharp. 'Now maybe you'd better leave. I'm not sure how much longer I can hold this tigress down.'

'Makes me sick just to see you touch her,' Mel snarled. 'Tell you what, Smith, if you're so sweet and innocent, how about letting me have a little look around that cabin of yours?'

'Not without a search warrant, you won't,' John said firmly.

'There, you see?' Mel said triumphantly to Lauren. 'He's afraid to let me in there.'

John shook his head. 'Not afraid, Cranston. Just not about to have my civil rights violated by a jealous suitor. Besides, I don't trust you as far as I could throw an elephant. I wouldn't be surprised if there's something in one of your pockets right now that you'd try to plant on me when no one was looking.'

Mel's face went pale. 'Why, you lousy . . . are you accusing me of being a crooked officer of the law?'

'I merely suggested that it was possible,' John replied smoothly. He removed his arm from Lauren's shoulders and took a step towards Mel. 'Of course, if it isn't, you won't mind if I search you thoroughly, will you?'

'Don't you touch me!' Mel said, his face going from white to red in a flash. He turned and went out of the pantry door, then stopped and glared back at John. 'Just you wait. As soon as Judge Peckinpaw is back in town, I'll get a warrant to search this whole place.

If you're smart, you'll be on your way before that happens.' With that, he whirled and strode rapidly out of the kitchen.

'Cheapskate,' Lauren muttered after him. 'That's the last free meal he gets here.' She looked up at John. 'Do you really think he'd try to plant something and then accuse you?'

'You're damned right I do,' John replied. 'If he does get a warrant, both of us are going to be with him every second. I don't ever want to be in a position where it's his word against mine.'

Lauren sank down in a chair at the big kitchen work-table and buried her face in her hands. Her head throbbed as if it were going to explode. 'What a day,' she groaned.

'Did Mel say some more bad things about John?' Brian asked, coming to stand beside her.

'I'm afraid so,' Lauren replied.

'He's the bad person,' Brian said loudly. 'I hate him.'

'No, you don't,' Lauren said, raising her head and putting her arm around Brian. 'Mel's not really bad. He's just confused and unhappy.' She looked over at John. 'Isn't he?'

'I wish I knew the answer to that,' he replied. He watched Lauren rubbing her aching forehead. 'Brian, why don't you put your mother to bed for a change tonight? She's tired and she has a headache. Have her take two aspirin, and then read her a little story.'

Brian's eyes grew wide. He looked first at John, and then at Lauren. 'Can I do that, Mommy?' he asked. 'Will it make you feel better if I do?'

'That,' Lauren said, giving John a grateful smile,

'would make me feel wonderful. Are you sure you and Isobel can handle everything here?' She heard Isobel's throaty chuckle behind her. 'Yes, I guess you can,' she said.

Lauren fell asleep almost as soon as Brian had carefully tucked her covers around her. She could only vaguely hear the sound of his high little voice, reciting his well-learned story of *Peter Rabbit*. She thought she felt a cool hand on her forehead, and the brush of soft lips against her cheek, but was not sure whether it was real or only a dream.

She slept as if she had been drugged, and awoke in the morning to bright sunlight flashing a pine-speckled pattern on her wall and the sound of her typewriter clicking rapidly in the next room.

'Good lord, what time is it?' she muttered, pushing herself up on one elbow and peering at her clock. Nine o'clock! Good heavens! What was wrong with everyone? They had let her oversleep by three hours! She sat up quickly, starting to swing her feet towards the edge of the bed. As if she were suspended in some kind of space capsule, the floor seemed suddenly to try to change places with the ceiling. With a groan, Lauren laid back down and closed her eyes, her head again throbbing unmercifully.

'You groaned?' asked a deep voice, tinged with amusement.

Lauren opened her eyes again and watched John cross the room and come to sit on the edge of her bed. 'I feel awful,' she said sulkily. 'What makes you so jolly? I shouldn't be here. I should be attending to business. What's going on? Where's Brian?'

'Would you rather I wept and beat my breast

because you've got the flu?' John asked, still smiling. 'When I felt your head last night it was as hot as Isobel's frying pan. I knew you were going to need to stay in bed this morning, so I had Isobel call her niece Nancy to come and help out. Her niece brought a friend, so I'm free to type those letters to send out. Brian's feeding Horse at the moment. How does your throat feel?'

'Terrible,' Lauren answered, swallowing painfully. 'I'd better get some medicine for this. I can't spend all day in bed.'

'Yes, you can,' John said firmly. 'The doctor's stopping by around noon. I expect he'll say the same thing, so don't frown at me like that. I can see that you're a rotten patient.'

'I hate being sick,' Lauren grumbled. 'I hate being useless.'

John grinned. 'You're not useless, you're very decorative. I can't think of anything nicer to look at than a bed with you in it. Now go back to sleep. Everything's under control.'

Lauren closed her eyes. John obviously did have everything running like clockwork. He did it so easily. A little place like Stoney Creek Lodge was no challenge at all to his talents, whereas it took everything she had to keep it going at all. It was bad enough feeling so rotten, without finding out that you weren't really needed after all, Lauren thought morosely. Tears trickled from the corners of her eyes.

'When you're through here,' she sniffed, 'why don't you go and run General Motors? That shouldn't be any problem for you, either.'

'You are *really* sick,' John said, caressing her

forehead gently. 'I hate that kind of work, remember? Besides, they haven't asked me lately. Now, get to sleep so you'll get better. I can't go on for long without you. It's no fun.'

Lauren blinked her eyes open and looked at John through the shimmer of her tears. John was so understanding. His face was such a wonderful combination of strength and gentleness. There was a soft warmth in his beautiful blue eyes that said clearly that he meant what he said. 'I'll be better by tomorrow. I promise,' Lauren said huskily.

'That's my girl,' John said, smiling. He bent and kissed her cheek. 'I'd better get back to work. Those letters need to go out today.'

Lauren watched him cross the room, tall and straight, his bearing dignified and regal. Even his well-worn clothing did not detract from his compelling presence. Was it only because she knew him better that he seemed so different now? she wondered. Or was it more than that? Was it because just having him near made her feel safe and warm and happy? Was it because . . . she loved him?

John paused at the door and looked back at her. 'Is there anything I can bring you?' he asked.

'No, thank you,' Lauren replied softly. John had already brought more into her life than she would have dreamed possible only a few short days ago. It remained for her to decide what to do about it. She did love him. The glow of happiness at his presence, at the deep, soft tones of his voice, reached her from across the room and ignited a little fire of longing in spite of how terrible she felt. She wanted him always close, always beside her, where she could touch him and hold him and feel his arms around her. She had felt that way about Paul, too. And then . . .

I can't always think about that, Lauren thought, turning her face to her pillow. She would have to learn to face life squarely again, with all of its uncertainties. But now, while she felt as if her body was a trembling mass of fever and pain, was not the time. When she felt better, she would make herself look at the problem and start to overcome it. She could do it. Others had.

CHAPTER SIX

IT WAS two days before Lauren was up and around, still feeling rather limp, but unwilling to let others continue to do her work for her. Being pampered had not been, she readily admitted to herself, an unpleasant experience. For the first time in many years, she had felt completely free of any responsibilities. Unfortunately, having John treat her like a fragile princess did nothing to ease her mind or heart. Awakening to find his smiling face looking down at her only made her fall ever more deeply in love with him. She had to get back into her routine and get her mind to functioning properly again, so that she could learn to cope with her new revelation. It wouldn't be fair to John to tell him, and then vacillate back and forth on the future because she was afraid. She had to overcome that problem first.

'Don't overdo it,' John said sternly, watching her bustle about, making a list of items to buy at the grocery in Crook's Crossing.

'Don't be so bossy,' Lauren retorted. 'If you and Brian don't stop fussing over me, I'll become totally useless.'

'You might put bubble gum on your list,' John suggested.

'Bubble gum?' Lauren stared at John. 'Grown men don't chew bubble gum.'

'This one does,' John replied with a chuckle. 'I took

it up when I quit smoking. I promised Brian I'd teach him to blow bubbles.'

Lauren shook her head. John was a never-ending series of surprises. 'All right, bubble gum it is,' she said, writing it down. 'Anything else?'

'A few things from the hardware store,' John said, handing her a list. 'Now that you're better, I've got to get moving on the repairs to the cabin. I expect we'll be getting some results from those advertisements pretty soon.'

'I hope so,' Lauren replied. If only the plan worked and she could keep the lodge, then she and John . . . She arrested the thought before it could run its course, but that did not stop the knot that formed in her midsection. She mustn't think that way, she warned herself. She must not let too much hinge on whether she could keep the lodge or not. Trying to make herself willing to accept the uncertainties of the future enough to be willing to make a commitment to John was problem enough. It was hard to let go of the dream that she and Paul had shared, but realistically the only thing to do was to keep busy, take one day at a time, and see what happened. 'Come on, Brian,' she said, trying to follow her own advice, 'let's go to town. We've got to get John all of these nails and things so you can help him.'

'And the bubble gum?' Brian asked hopefully.

'And the bubble gum,' Lauren promised.

It was over two hours later when Lauren returned, the jeep laden with bags of groceries and the boxes of nails and electrical repair items that John had ordered. The sight of Mel's police car parked in front of the lodge sent a chill of nervousness through her. Could he already have got that search warrant he had threatened to get? If so, she thought, as she lifted a heavy bag of groceries from the jeep, he could just wait and help her carry in the groceries before they started on that ridiculous search.

As if in answer to her thoughts, Mel appeared on the porch of the lodge and then hurried down the steps towards her. Instead of carrying an official-looking paper, he was clutching a bouquet in one hand.

'Here, let me have that,' he said, reaching for the bag and thrusting the flowers towards Lauren at the same time. 'I brought you these. I heard you'd been sick and I . . . I came to apologise for the other night.'

'Why, thank you, Mel,' Lauren said, touched by the look of anxiety on Mel's round, boyish face. 'I guess I should apologise, too. I got a little more upset than I should have.'

'You were probably coming down with the flu,' Mel said with a little smile. 'People get more upset when they aren't feeling good.'

'That could be what it was,' Lauren agreed. She followed Mel into the kitchen and found a vase for the bouquet of snapdragons and marigolds. 'These are beautiful,' she told him. 'I was . . . I was afraid you were here with that search warrant.'

'Oh, that,' Mel's face clouded. 'I'll tell you about that business in a minute. You sit down. I'll get the rest of the groceries. You want to help, Brian?'

'I'll take John his nails and stuff,' Brian said.

'Nails?' Mel questioned, frowning. 'Guess he's finally getting down to doing some repairs.'

'A lot of repairs,' Lauren replied, ignoring Mel's

implication that John had been shirking his work. 'He's going to get that cabin ready for occupancy. I've sent out advertisements to newspapers all over northern California, I'm hoping to need all three cabins fairly often.'

Mel nodded. 'Can't do any harm. I've always heard it pays to advertise.'

Lauren breathed a sigh of relief. At least Mel hadn't told her it was stupid to try it. If he had, she might have gone for that ketchup bottle again.

'You said you'd tell me something about the search warrant,' she reminded Mel when he had carried in the last bag of groceries. When he again looked hesitant, she suggested, 'Let's go down to my apartment and talk about it.' Whatever it is, she mused as they walked the short distance across the lodge, Mel was not very happy about it. 'Have you run into some kind of problem?' she asked as soon as they were sitting in her sunny living-room.

Mel made a wry face. 'Yeah, I guess you could call it that. Some Federal agents showed up yesterday and arrested a couple of guys who were living in an abandoned shack in the canyon behind Crook's Crossing. Said they were the ones who had been doing the dealing in this area. They'd been on their trail for a long time.'

'Then you no longer suspect John?'

'Well . . . I guess not. He still looks suspicious to me, but I gave the Feds a complete description of him and his background, and they said he wasn't on their list. I don't know how they think they can keep track of everyone, but they seemed real positive he wasn't anyone they wanted. So that means I couldn't get a search warrant anyway. Unless some more illegal stuff shows up in these parts.'

'I'm very glad to hear that those men were caught,' Lauren said quietly, 'and not just because of John. I don't like the idea of such things going on so close to home.'

Privately, she wondered if the reason the Federal agents had been so positive that John was not someone they wanted was that they knew exactly who he was and why he was here. That thought had not, of course, occurred to Mel. Since John had asked her not to mention anything to Mel about the fact that he had a reason for being here, she would not do so, but Mel's report made her more curious than ever about John's mysterious reason. He had said it had nothing to do with Mel's accusation, yet the Federal agents appeared on the scene only a short time after John had made his tour of the logging roads. Was there really no connection? Or was he perhaps some other kind of a government agent, involved in something even more dangerous, who had simply passed on some information that he gleaned on another topic? If it was dangerous . . .

'You still seem kind of down in the dumps,' Mel commented, interrupting Lauren's musings. 'Are you still feeling poorly?'

'Oh, not really,' she replied, trying to smile brightly. 'I just have a lot on my mind. I'm trying to figure out how to get ready for what I hope will be a flood of new visitors.'

'I hope it will, too,' Mel said quickly. 'I know how much this places means to you, and if I can help at all, just say the word. Well, I'd better get back to work.

Got a new deputy to break in.'

'Thanks again for the flowers, Mel,' Lauren said as she followed him to the door. 'I accept your apology. But don't you think you owe John one, too? You were terribly unpleasant to him, you know.'

Mel gave Lauren a sideways glance. 'I suppose so. But I still don't like having him hanging around here, and it's not just because of you. I've got a funny feeling about him. There's something more going on with him than he's telling.'

That was so close to the mark that Lauren almost shivered. Instead she shrugged. 'I can't imagine what, Mel,' she said. 'He's been working his head off for me most of the time.'

'Well, you keep a sharp eye on him,' Mel replied, 'and let me know if you hear or see anything suspicious.'

'I will,' Lauren promised soberly.

She went back to work, feeling relieved that she and Mel were on reasonably good terms again, but still disturbed by her earlier thoughts. Could John's reasons for coming to this particular area have some element of danger? Now that she knew him better, she could tell that he would meet danger with the same calm, unflinching courage that Paul had done. She did not want to spend her life always wondering from day to day if her husband was going to meet disaster and not come home again. Maybe if she asked John outright if he was frequently involved in dangerous situations, he might give her a straight answer. On the other hand, if he was like Paul, he might not really see them as necessarily life-threatening. He would only smile that amused little smile of his and say calmly, 'Of course not.' Lauren sighed heavily. There was, of course, one other possibility that she should consider. Paul and John were alike in many ways. Maybe that was the only kind of man she could fall in love with!

'That's probably the trouble,' she muttered to herself, peering into a drawer where she was sure she had stored an extra tablecloth.

'Talking to yourself, ma'am?' came a deep Texas drawl from behind her.

'Yep,' Lauren replied, turning to face John's teasing smirk. 'What is this, the cowboy's return?' She looked down at Brian, who was standing beside him. 'Your pardner's kind of small, mister,' she said. 'I hope you aren't planning to hold up a bank.'

'No, ma'am,' John drawled. 'But we were planning on takin' a little ride, if you don't mind. We've been workin' mighty hard all day. It's time for a break.'

'Sounds good to me,' Lauren said. 'Have fun.'

'We will. You'll have to come and check our progress later,' John said in his normal voice. Then he bent and whispered in Lauren's ear, 'Mel didn't give you any more trouble, did he?'

Lauren shook her head. 'Quite to the contrary. I'll tell you about it tonight.' She watched the tall, dark man and the small blond boy walk off side by side and shook her head again. That was another good reason to love John Smith and to be willing to face whatever uncertainties a life with him might hold. He was the kind of man she would like her son to be when he grew up.

That night, when Lauren told John what Mel had told her, he did not seem especially surprised.

'The Drug Enforcement Agency has a pretty good network in this area,' he said.

'I'm sure they do,' Lauren said drily. 'Are you sure it's a coincidence that you appeared only a few days before they did?'

John chuckled. 'Positive,' he said.

'That's what I thought you'd say,' Lauren said with a sigh. 'Can you . . . can you at least tell me if there's anything dangerous about the reason you're here?'

John got up from his chair, and came to sit beside Lauren on the sofa, where she had been resting at his insistence. He took her hands in his and held them tightly. 'Angel,' he said, 'there's an element of danger in just being alive. I could be forgetful or sloppy and electrocute myself while I'm working on the wiring in that cabin. But I won't, because I'm careful, and I know what I'm doing. I know that having Paul killed as he was has made the world look frightening and insecure to you, and it may take you a while longer to get over those fears. But you have to learn to believe in yourself and your abilities to handle the situations you'll find yourself involved in. Otherwise, you'll never do anything worthwhile. And, of course, you have to believe at least a little bit that Lady Luck is on your side. She certainly was when I found you.'

Lauren studied John's face, the intense, bright blue of his eyes so startlingly vivid, even in the dim light of one small lamp. He said he felt lucky to have met her. She was at least twice as lucky to have met him. She smiled ruefully. 'I think maybe I'm the lucky one,' she said. 'I'm trying to get over being such a coward.'

'I know,' John said softly. 'I can see you struggling with it sometimes.' His eyes scanned Lauren's face and then settled on her lips. 'I wonder. Will it make it easier or harder if I kiss you more often? I've been trying to decide . . .' He brushed his hand gently across Lauren's cheek and then tucked it behind her neck, watching her carefully, a slightly questioning look in his eyes.

'I don't know,' Lauren breathed, feeling her heart begin to race in anticipation. 'Maybe there's only one way to find out.'

The questioning look vanished into one of intense happiness. John's arms closed around Lauren, his mouth finding hers with such a burst of passion that she melted against him, clutching him to her with all of her strength. Spontaneously their lips parted, their tongues darting and seeking each other hungrily. As if by mutual understanding, they shifted to stretch out together on the sofa. The feeling of John's long, hard body against hers kindled long-dormant fires of longing that sent Lauren's hands searching and caressing in their desire to know all of this man. John responded, cupping her breasts, delicately grasping their swollen peaks, until Lauren groaned softly at the ecstasy she felt. She moved to help him unfasten her silk blouse, but he stayed her hand and raised his head.

'Not yet, angel,' he said softly. 'Some day soon, but not tonight.' He smiled at Lauren's hurt, confused expression. 'I have only so much self-control,' he said, 'and it's already being severely tested. Lord knows I want to make love to you, but not until you're as sure of how you feel about me as I am that I love you. I don't think you are.'

Lauren looked away. She was sure. More than ever.

The only thing that she was unsure of was whether she could follow her heart. If they were to make love before she knew the answer to that question, she would not feel really free to give herself to John completely. That wouldn't be fair to him. And it would only make her decision more difficult, confusing physical passion with abiding love. John, as usual, was right, as far as he knew. She looked up at him and made a face.

'I guess you're right,' she said. 'Sort of.'

'Sort of?' John raised a quizzical eyebrow. 'What do you mean "sort of"?'

Lauren smiled what she hoped was a mysterious smile. 'You have your secrets and I'll have mine,' she said.

'Aha! Playing games,' John said, giving Lauren a knowing look. He sat up and tossed his head back with a characteristic gesture. 'Two can do that. I have another secret myself, which I will reveal to you some evening when you're in an especially good humour.'

'Tell me now,' Lauren said. 'I'm in a very good humour.'

John shook his head. 'Not good enough for this one,' he teased. 'Besides, I think you'd better get to bed early. We wouldn't want you to have a relapse. I think we'll be getting some results from these advertisements very soon.'

No matter how much Lauren pleaded, John remained maddeningly adamant. 'The phone had better start ringing off the hook tomorrow,' she warned him at last, 'or else I'm going to be furious with you.'

'It will,' John replied confidently.

His prophecy was almost correct. Two days later, the first calls that were directly linked to the newspaper advertisments came in. Lauren was ecstatic.

'We've got two of the cabins rented for next weekend,' she announced triumphantly, shortly after breakfast. By late afternoon, there were several new arrivals taking rooms at the lodge. They had seen the posters. Only two more days, and John announced at dinnertime that his cabin was ready for occupancy.

'Can I see it now?' Lauren asked impatiently. He had forbidden her to visit during the last few days, pleading that he wanted to surprise her.

'After dinner,' John agreed.

When Brian had been tucked in for the night, John took Lauren's hand, and together they walked to his cabin in the crisp night air. 'It feels like autumn tonight,' John commented.

'It's almost here. It won't be long until it snows.' Lauren sighed. 'We still don't have many reservations for after Labor Day, but . . .' Her voice trailed off as John opened the door and turned on the light. 'John, it's beautiful! When did you do all of this?' she cried, amazed. 'And,' she demanded, 'where did you get the money for that panelling? And everything else?' For the walls were now covered in pine panelling, a colonial chandelier hung from the ceiling, and on the floor was an obviously good quality flooring which mimicked inlaid brick so successfully that for a moment Lauren thought it was the real thing. Besides that, the kitchen bar stools had been painted, and there were now two comfortable chairs in addition to the old wooden chairs that had been refinished.

John chuckled. 'I had some money with me from my last job. I wasn't hitch-hiking because I was broke. Only because it seemed like the best way to get where I was going at the time.'

Lauren stared at him and shook her head. 'I don't know what to say, John, except thank you,' she said. 'Of course, I'll pay . . .' She stopped. John was watching her intently, a little frown starting between his dark brows. He obviously did not want to hear her say that she would pay him back. He had done it because he wanted to help someone he loved, whose future he was determined to share. Lauren smiled. 'It's beautiful,' she said again. 'Is this that secret you mentioned?'

'That's better,' John said, looking both relieved and amused. 'No, this isn't the secret. But I guess you deserve to find out about my secret vice.' He gestured towards one of the new chairs. 'Sit down and I'll get my guitar.'

'I've been wondering if you ever played it,' Lauren said, taking a seat in one of the new chairs.

John grinned. 'You may soon wonder why,' he said. He brought out his guitar and draped his long frame comfortably over one of the bar stools. While he proceeded to tune it, he said, 'I call this song "When Jenny Went Away".'

'You write your own music?' Lauren said, surprised.

'No, I just work it out,' John replied, testing a few chords. 'I make up a song and then find the chords to go with it by trial and error.' He played a melodic sequence of single notes and then began.

It only took Lauren a few moments to realise that

John had an exceptional talent. His voice was as beautiful as she had remembered, the song touching and lovely. It was a ballad about a young man who loved a beautiful but fickle girl. She left him for another man, whose love was as inconstant as hers, with tragic results.

When John finished, Lauren applauded loudly. 'That was wonderful,' she said. 'You're far too modest about your talent.'

'Thank you ma'am,' John drawled. 'My horse liked it, too. I had a lot of trouble with the words, at first, making them come out phrased just right.'

'You definitely succeeded,' Lauren said. 'It was so haunting. The story reminds me a little of that English ballad "Barbara Allen", where the two lovers end up buried side by side.'

'I guess it could be compared to that,' John said, giving Lauren a strange little half-smile. 'I never thought of it that way.' He strummed a few more chords. 'I really wanted you to hear something I've been working on lately.'

'Lately? How did you ever find time to do that and finish the cabin, too?' Lauren asked.

'I do it while I'm working on other things,' John replied. 'It keeps my mind occupied. I call this "Mountain Lovesong". It's about us. That's why it's not really finished yet.' He lowered his head, struck a minor chord, and then began to sing, his voice deep and soft and warm:

"In mountains cold with lonely paths
Where fears still followed sorrow,
The light of love came into view
My heart longed for tomorrow.

I sent it forth with warmth and hope
To face its certain capture,
And find a home where love could grow
For all the days ever after.'

Lauren was so moved that she could scarcely speak when John had finished. 'It's so . . . so beautiful that I could cry,' she said huskily. 'But why do you say it's not finished?'

'It needs another verse,' John replied softly, his eyes searching Lauren's face as he spoke. 'It's not clear what happens to that captured heart. Has it really found the home it sought, with another heart to share it?'

'Oh.' Lauren said, looking down. What could she say? She was still not sure what she was going to do, and now John was apparently growing tired of waiting for her to make up her mind. She looked at him pleadingly. 'I'm afraid I still don't have the answer to that. I've had so much to think about lately, and I still feel all tied up in knots over what's going to happen to the lodge. I've tried to tell myself not to attach too much importance to that, but now that it seems there might be some hope . . .'

'Don't get upset. I'm not worried about your answer,' John said calmly. 'Just take your time. I don't want to put extra pressure on you and make things more difficult for you.'

Lauren could see the disappointment in John's face, in spite of his comforting words. 'You aren't!' she exclaimed. 'I could never have done any of this without you.' She smiled ruefully. 'I don't suppose I could persuade you to play for the guests? You're so good that people would come from miles around to hear you, once the word got out.'

John shook his head. 'I'm afraid not. As I said, it's my secret vice, and I want to keep it that way. Besides, I think your evaluation may be a little biased.'

'I don't think so,' Lauren replied, surprised at John's reticence. 'I'm positive that you're good enough for there to be no real reason for you to be shy about playing in front of other people.'

'I'm not shy. I just don't want to do it,' John said firmly.

'I think it amounts to the same thing,' Lauren retorted.

'If that's the way you see it,' he said, an irritated tone in his voice. He stood up and put his guitar away. 'I think we'd better call it a night. We're both tired and on edge.' He followed Lauren as she went towards the door. 'I'll take the jeep into town in the morning, if you don't mind,' he said. 'I want to get a few things to fix up a place for me to sleep in Horse's stable.'

'In the stable?'

'I've got to sleep somewhere,' John replied.

So that was why John was cross, Lauren thought. He had hoped that after seeing the cabin and hearing his song she might declare her love and invite him to share her bed. 'I guess that's right,' she said, annoyed that John would stoop to such tactics. 'I'll see you at breakfast, then.'

'Right,' John said brusquely. 'Goodnight.'

'Goodnight.' Lauren walked back to the lodge alone, feeling depressed. Something had gone wrong, and she was not quite sure what it was. It wasn't like John to pressure her like that. Didn't he think she was appreciative enough of what he'd done? Was he upset because she suggested he play his music in public? Or was it all because she hadn't been ready to make any declaration of love? She took a deep breath, and let it out in a huge sigh. She was doing the best she could, working eighteen hours a day, trying to make things come together. John should understand that. He usually did. Maybe he was right. They were both just tired. Things would be back on an even keel in the morning.

But they were not. John was late getting back from his trip to town, and he remained tight-lipped and uncommunicative. In the afternoon he went off for a long ride. By dinnertime, he did seem to be in a better humour, Lauren noted, actually smiling at her once or twice. After dinner, he asked Lauren if she would like to go for a walk.

'Maybe tomorrow night,' she replied, shaking her head. 'I'm exhausted. I'll get things organised better soon.' She smiled, but this time John did not smile back. He shrugged coolly and walked away. Her heart sank, but she felt a little twinge of annoyance, too. If something was bothering John, the least he could do was come out with it. She hated feeling as if she'd done something wrong, but not knowing what it might be. Tomorrow she would have to take the bull by the horns and ask him what it was.

But the next day produced a minibus filled with senior citizens who wanted to stay for several days, and on top of the extra guests, Isobel's niece, Nancy, who had been helping regularly, had the flu and sent a friend instead. That meant showing the new girl what to do.

'I'm beginning to feel like a whirling dervish,'

Lauren commented to John, when they met in the hallway in the middle of the afternoon. 'I'm not sure I'm ready for so much success.'

'It can be a mixed blessing,' he commented drily.

Lauren frowned. John still looked withdrawn, as if he were brooding over something. 'John,' she said slowly, 'I can't help feeling that you're angry with me, and I don't know why. If something's wrong, I do wish you'd tell me what it is.'

'I'm not angry with you,' he replied, his voice very low. 'I just have a lot on my mind.'

'Can't you tell me about it?' Lauren pleaded. She hated the way the blank, expressionless face before her made her feel. She loved John but, if he wouldn't talk to her, how could she help?

'Maybe later,' he said, then turned and walked away, leaving Lauren staring after him, an ache in her heart.

Lauren tried several more times during the days that followed to find out what was bothering John, but could get no satisfactory answer. She began to wonder if Mel could have been right, that whatever John was hiding about his reason for coming to this part of the Cascade Mountains was something criminal, or at least something he had begun to think twice about ever revealing to her. If that was the case, he might have begun regretting his declaration of love, and his vow to spend the rest of his life with her. For they surely could never marry with some dark secret hanging between them?

Nevertheless, when Mel came in one day, plonked himself down in the middle of the confusion of the kitchen at lunchtime, devoured a piece of pie and then proceeded to ask, 'How much longer is Smith going to hang around? I should think you'd be tired of him freeloading off you by now. He must have all the repairs made, or is he still dragging them out?' Lauren exploded.

'As far as I'm concerned,' she snapped, 'John can stay here forever. For your information, he's the one who got my bookkeeping straightened out and most of the advertising was his idea. He's earned a lot more than I can ever repay!'

Mel only looked sullen. 'The guy's a regular genius, isn't he?' he growled. 'Doesn't it make you kind of curious about why he's playing handyman when he doesn't have to?'

'Maybe because he wants to,' Lauren replied coldly, suddenly wishing that she had not said so much. Still, she couldn't imagine how having Mel know that he had some other talents could do John any harm, aside from making Mel suspicious. That shouldn't matter. He was already that.

Lauren thought of telling John what she had told Mel, and asking him if it was going to present any problems, but John grew more and more taciturn day by day, until she felt as if an invisible wall had grown up between them. He kept at his work and was still warm and kind to Brian, but he was little more than politely civil to her, responding to whatever directions she gave him with only a nod, and answering her questions with short, terse replies. Sometimes when she flew past him on the way from one chore to another she would see him watching her, his expression stoic and unreadable. Even the fact that most of the rooms and all three cabins were now filled through the Labor Day weekend brought her little joy, even though she frequently reminded herself how thrilled Paul would be if he could see what had happened. The only saving grace, she thought more than once, was that she had no time to brood during the day and she fell into bed at night too exhausted to do anything but fall asleep. At last, even exhaustion was not enough, and she would lie in her bed, tossing and turning, wondering what she had done to turn John against her.

One night, as she sat on the edge of her bed, staring into the darkness and trying to decide if she might not be better off staying up all night, she thought she heard the sounds of John's guitar wafting through her windows on the light breeze. It was a mournful sound, but the melody was familiar. He was playing the song he had written for the two of them "Mountain Lovesong". Suddenly, a deep sob burst from Lauren's throat and she buried her face in her hands. Why had she asked him to play for the guests? That had been so stupid of her. Maybe that was the reason he was still angry. He had meant that song for her ears only, something special to be treasured. What was the other song? Oh, yes. "When Jenny Went Away". A song about a girl . . .

Lauren's head jerked up. Of course! That song was telling a story, too, and she had been so wrapped up in her own problems that she hadn't realised it. Jenny must have been someone real, someone whom John had loved! He was trying to tell her that he understood how she felt about Paul. It must still be so painful to him that he could only bring himself to tell the story in song. The pain was there, in the beginning of "Mountain Lovesong", too, in the words that spoke of lonely paths, where fear still followed sorrow. Oh, why hadn't she listened, really listened, and understood?

In a flash, Lauren had slipped into her warm robe and slippers. She started out of the door, then stopped. What was she going to do? What was she going to say? Would it really help to go to John in the middle of the night and tell him that she understood what he had been trying to tell her about Jenny now? Perhaps she had better think it through a little more before she tried to talk to him again. Maybe tomorrow, after dinner, would be a better time. Reluctantly, she took off her robe and crawled back beneath her blankets. Yes, tomorrow she would definitely have a long talk with John.

But John was nowhere to be found the next evening after dinner. The following day was Friday, and the Labor Day guests began to arrive. Then the rest of the early September holiday came and went in a blur of activity. On Tuesday evening after Brian was in bed, John came to the door of Lauren's apartment and announced that he wanted to talk to her.

'Of course,' Lauren said, a wave of anxiety sending a sudden shiver through her. John looked so serious. She began to chatter, hoping for some kind of cue that would tell her why John had come. 'Come in and sit down. I . . . I've been wanting to talk to you, too, but we haven't had much chance to talk lately, have we? I've been so tired at night . . .' She tried to smile brightly, but felt as if she were only baring her teeth. 'I guess there's such a thing as too much success all at once. At first it made me sleep well, but lately I've been having trouble sleeping.' There was no response from John, no flicker of light in his eyes. Fighting down a feeling of panic, Lauren turned quickly and crossed the room. She sat down on her sofa and patted the cushion beside her. 'Sit down. I'm sure you're tired, too.'

'No, thanks,' John said. He paced back and forth across the room several times, his hands thrust deep in his pockets. At last he stopped in front of Lauren and looked down at her, his face deeply sad. 'I'm afraid I'm going to have to leave in a couple of days, Lauren,' he said.

CHAPTER SEVEN

'LEAVE?' Lauren could scarcely get the word out over the sudden constriction that clutched at her throat.

'That's right.' John bit his lip. 'I don't know quite how to say this, but I think I've evaluated the situation correctly so I'll be as brief as possible. I realise now that the lodge, and your memories of Paul, are more important to you than I could ever be. I don't blame you for that. It's not something you can do anything about, I'm afraid. I don't seem to be making any progress on the other reason I came here, so I think it's time I was moving on.'

'B-but I don't want you to leave,' Lauren stammered, staring at him through a shimmer of tears.

'Really?' John's mouth twisted into a wry smile. 'For the last few weeks you haven't seemed to care whether I was here or not.'

'But I've been so busy . . . and you've hardly talked to me at all,' Lauren protested. 'I thought you were angry with me, after that night when you showed me the cabin and sang for me.'

'I wasn't. But when I came in the next morning and said good morning to you, all you did was snap at me that I was late. Every time I've tried to start a conversation, you've put me off. Too busy now, you say. And you'll keep right on being busy, because if you're to pay your mortgage you have to. I don't think

I'm willing to take what's left over.'

'But you're the one who got me to advertise!' Lauren angrily dashed the tears from her cheeks. 'You're not being fair. You haven't wanted to talk when I have, either.'

John sighed. 'I know. I admit it's partly my falt. You wanted it so badly, and I wanted to help. But it's your dream, not mine. I watch you running here and there, working so hard, but you don't come and ask for my help, you demand it. You can't take time just to be with me. I don't feel a part of it any more. I still love you, though, and I probably always will. I hope for your sake that you succeed here and find someone to share it with some day.' He paused, his head bowed. 'I—I don't quite know how to break the news to Brian.'

Lauren stared at him, his words echoing around and around inside what felt like a cold, empty shell. *Someone, some day. Break the news to Brian.* Until that moment, she had not really believed that John menat to go. But he couldn't go. She loved him! She leaped to her feet and flung herself into John's arms with such force that he stumbled backwards, his arms going around her reflexively. 'You can't go, John,' she cried. 'I love you!' John only stared at her, his expression unchanged. 'Didn't you hear me?' she said frantically, clutching at him with her hands.

'I heard you,' he replied. He shook himself free and went to stand by the window, gazing out into the softly lighted parking area in front of the lodge. 'I wonder,' he said, almost as if to himself, 'what it is that made you come to that conclusion so suddenly? Is it because you know how unhappy Brian will be if I leave?'

'No!' Lauren said vehemently. She went to John's side and took hold of his arm, wanting desperately to hold on to him, to be able to feel his strength while she tried to think how to tell him what she truly felt. 'Please,' she said, 'give me a chance to explain. Of course I care about how Brian feels, but . . .' She stopped and tugged at his arm. 'Come and sit down. I have a lot of other things to tell you.' She felt as if her heart had stopped while she waited for some response.

'All right,' John said at last. He turned and walked swiftly to sit down in one of the straight chairs by Lauren's table.

'Sit over here,' Lauren said, pointing to the sofa. 'I don't want you over there where you can try not to look at me.' Her adrenalin was beginning to flow, and with it her determination that John was not going to leave until he had heard, and understood, everything she had to say.

John's mouth tightened into a straight, uncompromising line, but he got up and moved to the spot Lauren had indicated. She sat down beside him, studying his face intently. It was still as expressionless as a face that was lined from smiles and frowns could be, but she thought she detected a faint flicker of response in the dark depths of eyes that could be so dazzlingly bright and warm. Gathering all of her courage, she looked down and took one of John's long hands between hers, then raised her chin and looked him squarely in the eyes, her heart pounding but her voice steady.

'I don't know quite how to tell you everything that I . . . I probably should have told you a long time ago,' she said. 'I—I'm sorry that I was so busy and short with you. I guess I didn't even realise I was. It certainly didn't mean what you thought it did. The lodge does mean a lot to me, and so do my memories of Paul, but I've realised for some time that I can't live in the past. It's been wonderful having so many people here and knowing that I may be able to keep the lodge, thanks to you, but . . . it hasn't been any fun. Not the way I thought it would be. All the time you've been thinking I was ignoring you, I've been wondering why you haven't been talking to me. It's taken most of the pleasure out of the success for me. Without you here, I wouldn't care what happened to the lodge.'

'Now, wait a minute, Lauren,' John said seriously, his hand tightening around hers, 'I don't believe that. It will always mean a lot to you, whether I'm here or not. Perhaps I should have found a more tactful way . . .'

'Oh, stop it, John!' Lauren interrupted impatiently. 'You still think that I just discovered that I love you when you threatened to leave. Well, I didn't. I've known for a long time that I love you very, very much. Ever since that time when I was sick, and you took such wonderful care of me. I didn't tell you then, because I was still afraid to follow where my heart wanted to lead, and I didn't want to say "I love you, but . . ." I knew that wasn't what you wanted to hear. So instead I kept waiting until I could be sure I wasn't afraid.'

'And suddenly, now that I'm about to leave, you're not?' John asked, tilting his head back and looking at Lauren through narrowed eyes.

'Oh, I'm still afraid,' Lauren said quickly. 'But I'm

more afraid of never having you than losing you. I think . . . I think you're afraid, too. The other night when I couldn't sleep, I thought I heard you playing your guitar and I remembered that song you sang about . . . about Jenny. I wish I'd understood sooner what it meant, but right then it came to me. You were trying to tell me that you lost someone, too! Maybe you're just as afraid of losing someone again as I am, except you tried to deal with it by telling me you loved me right away, hoping that if I loved you back it would help you to forget. But then, when you thought I didn't love you, you started to be afraid again.' She stopped, her heart sinking at the still withdrawn look in John's eyes. 'I . . . I guess I waited too long,' she added hoarsely, bowing her head and looking down at her hands.

John, too, looked down at Lauren's hands, clasped so tightly around his. He freed one hand, and with one finger he gently lifted her chin until her eyes met his. His eyes were moist, but glowing with the deepest fire she had ever seen.

'My wise, wonderful little golden-haired angel,' he said, his voice shaking with emotion, 'it could never, never be too late for you. I love you with all my heart, and I will for all eternity.' Then, in one swift move, he gathered her into his arms and crushed her against him. His lips trailed a path of kisses to her lips, his mouth closing over hers with a passion that left her breathless, clinging to him with a strength that came from the dawning realisation that John was not going away. He was going to be hers forever! Skyrockets of happiness burst in Lauren's heart. She abandoned herself to the sensations of wild excitement that flew through her at the eager explorations of John's hands. He seemed to want to touch every part of her, to know, too, that she was completely his. When at last he raised his head, he cradled her in his arms, his lips kissing her forehead, her cheeks, her hair. 'I guess both of us need to do a lot more talking from now on,' he said, pausing between kisses. 'You're right, I was afraid, and I still am. But if we talk about our fears together, they'll go away in time.' He gave a short little laugh. 'I probably should take my own advice. Do you know what bothered me the most?'

Lauren shook her head. 'No. Tell me.'

John touched the slender gold band that was still on her finger. 'You're still wearing your wedding band,' he said softly. 'I'd see you looking at it sometimes, when you didn't know I was watching, and I thought you were thinking about Paul and wishing he was here.'

'I was thinking about him,' Lauren said. 'I suppose in a way, I was wishing he was here. He would have been so happy to see the lodge doing so well. But I knew he couldn't be. Mostly I was trying to cheer myself up when I was feeling especially badly about how things were going between you and me.'

She lifted her hand in front of her and stared at the little circle of gold that had symbolised her commitment to Paul. To her it meant something beautiful that would live in her heart forever, but to John it symbolised something that kept them apart. Very slowly, with a trembling hand, she slid the ring from her finger and put it into the pocket of her blouse. She looked back at John, to see his eyes filled with tears, above the most loving smile she had ever seen.

Silently he took her hand in his and bent his dark head to softly kiss the place where her ring had been.

'I wish I had your courage,' John said, raising his head and looking deeply into Lauren's eyes. He held her hand against his cheek. 'Some day soon, you'll wear my wedding ring, but there are so many things I need to tell you first. It isn't going to be easy.'

'Do you mean about Jenny?' Lauren asked. She wanted John always to look happy, instead of worried as he did now. 'You don't need to tell me if its still too painful for you.'

'That's part of it,' John said. He touched his lips to Lauren's wrist and held them there for a moment, then smiled. 'But I can tell you about her without too much difficulty. She was lovely, young, and innocent . . . or so I thought. We met one summer at the beach, and fell in love. For over a year I courted her in the most traditional ways, always thinking that she was a sweet, virgin treasure. Then, one autumn afternoon . . .' John paused, a look of pain crossing his face, 'I found her at my parents' home, in my stepbrother's room, in bed with him.' He grimaced. 'That was the first real shock of my life, I think. I'd always been so lucky before. I tried to find it in my heart to forgive her, but I couldn't, especially after I found out that my stepbrother was far from the first. The second shock, of course, was when she died. My stepbrother got her pregnant, then refused to marry her. She had a botched abortion. If only she'd come to me, I'd have married her in spite of everything. But, of course, we'd said such terrible things to each other by then. . .'

John closed his eyes, and Lauren held him close, her

heart aching for his sorrow. 'It's strange how you blame yourself,' she said softly. 'I kept thinking of all of the things I could have done or said to keep Paul from going out that day. But he would have hated me if I'd interfered with what he thought he should do. And even if you'd never said those things and had married Jenny, I doubt you'd have been happy after what had happened.'

'I know,' John said, sighing deeply. 'If only a person could see into the future . . .' He lifted Lauren and turned her so that he could look into her eyes. 'There are some other things I'm going to have to tell you, a little later. But first, I have a problem to solve. You may be able to help me.'

'Does it have something to do with the reason you came here?' Lauren asked. 'The one you said you weren't making any progress on?'

John nodded, his expression very serious again. 'When I decided to leave, I'd pretty well decided to abandon what I was doing and just forget it. I was going to go back to Texas and be a cowhand again. I may as well confess that part of my reason for wanting to leave was that I began to feel that I couldn't simply answer the questions I set out to answer without telling you about it eventually. It's a personal quest, not something I'm doing for anyone else, even though I let you think it might be in hopes that I could find what I needed to know and then drop it, simply telling you my secret mission was accomplished. But that wouldn't be fair to you. There's too much risk that you might find out from someone else and hate me for not telling you myself, so I must be the one to tell you, even though it scares the very devil out of me to think of what you're going to say when you know the whole story. I am going to have to follow through and face it now, though. There's no other way.'

'Oh, John,' Lauren said, laying her hand alongside his cheek, 'I can't imagine anything you've done that would be that bad. Besides . . .' she smiled mischievously, 'maybe you could use a little less devil in you.'

'There are a number of people who would agree with you,' John said, smiling back at her and pulling her close to him again. 'No, I haven't done anything terrible, so don't worry about that. And I'll do my best to tell you everything in such a way that it doesn't shock you too much. But for now, let's just spend the rest of this evening snuggling and kissing and talking about pleasant things. We're both tired, and I have to tell you that I'm damned tired of sleeping with Horse. He snores and stamps his feet all night. Do you mind if I sleep on the sofa here tonight?'

'You can sleep with me in my bed if you want to,' Lauren replied, slipping her hand between the buttons of John's shirt and beginning to caress his chest. 'I think that would be even nicer. You may as well enslave me completely before you shock me with this great mystery of yours.'

'Mmm,' John sighed, stretching out and beginning some explorations of his own, his lips and tongue beginning to tease Lauren's ear and neck with devastating effect. 'I don't think we should do that,' he murmured, finding the corner of Lauren's mouth and tickling it with his tongue. 'I don't think there's any good way to explain to Brian why we're in bed together if we're not married, and some day he might throw that back at us when we least expect to hear it.'

'I suppose you're right,' Lauren said with a sigh, that turned into a groan as John slid his hand beneath her bra. 'Take my bra off,' she whispered against John's lips, beginning to pull his shirt free of his jeans.

'Oh, angel, I don't . . .' John began, then fell silent as Lauren pressed her lips to his, her tongue invading his mouth with little darting movements. She felt his hand reach back to unfasten her bra, then once again slide forward to push it away. Her breasts tingled beneath the touch of his hands. When he pinched the swollen peaks gently, she drew in her breath sharply, then reached down to unfasten the blouse that still came between them and fling it aside. John stroked her with feather-light fingers, his eyes never leaving hers. 'Are you very sure?' he asked.

'Very sure,' she whispered in reply.

John took off his shirt, then lay down beside her. He touched her cheek very softly with his lips, his fingertips trailing a delicate path along her body. Slowly, very slowly, his mouth moved towards hers. Lauren, lying as still as if she were in a trance, felt as if she were being treated to the most marvellously tender loving she had ever felt. Inside, a great warm core seemed to be building, sending signals to the outer world wherever John's fingers touched. When his mouth at last covered hers, it was like an explosion of heat, an experience so breathtaking that she gasped and dug her fingers into John's shoulders. Moments later she groaned and closed her eyes, watching the soaring flashes of light that danced before her eyelids while John's lips began a journey down her neck until they paused and tugged gently at her rosy nipples. His fingers traced a circle around her navel, then unfastened the waistband of her trousers and slipped inside. Floods of longing crashed through Lauren's body in waves, and she tugged John's jeans open and touched him lovingly.

'Oh, angel,' he groaned, pressing against her. 'I want you so much.' His hands moulded her eagerly to his thrusting hips, and he raised his head, his eyes, dark with desire, searching hers. 'If I take you now . . .' he said raggedly, his arms enfolding her more gently, 'damn it . . .' he buried his face momentarily against her hair, '. . . I won't feel right about it.' He raised his head again. 'Can you forgive me?' he asked, with a smile that was both sad and loving.

Lauren stared at him, aching with frustration but so enchanted by his smile that she could only nod. 'I suppose so,' she said, 'but I don't understand why you stopped. Is it just because we're not married yet?'

'That's a big "just because",' John said with a sigh, tickling Lauren's bare back as she lay still beside him. 'Not only because of Brian, but because when I make love to you for the first time, I want everything to be absolutely perfect. No loose ends, no problems, no questions nagging at the back of my mind. And that won't happen, I'm afraid, until the day you say "I do". Which, with any luck at all, will be very soon.'

'It had better be,' Lauren said with an exaggerated pout. She wriggled closer to John and laid her head on his shoulder, one arm thrown around him. 'Let's just go to sleep like this, then,' she murmured. 'Later on, one of us will probably wake up and can wander off to the bathroom. OK?'

'All right, angel,' John said with a chuckle. 'Torture me if you must. I can take it.'

'Wonderful,' Lauren said. She closed her eyes, wrapped in the warm strength of John's arms, drinking in the soft essence of his scent. It was, she thought in the few seconds before she fell asleep, a heavenly place to be.

CHAPTER EIGHT

SUNLIGHT and the smell of fresh coffee awakened Lauren in the morning. She opened her eyes to see Brian standing beside her bed, a cup of coffee in his hands. Behind him stood John, smiling down at her.

'Good morning, sleepyhead,' John said. 'We thought you deserved a little extra sleep this morning.'

'I appreciate it,' Lauren replied. She sat up, clutching the sheet around her as she became quickly aware that she still had nothing on above her waist. She held out her hand to Brian for the coffee. 'Thank you, love,' she said, taking a sip and looking at him questioningly over the top of her cup. 'Have you decided not to talk this morning?'

Brian nodded, his face pink from the effort.

'Hmm,' Lauren said, frowning. 'Have you got a secret you're not supposed to tell me?'

Brian nodded again.

John chuckled. 'It's not your mother you're not supposed to tell,' he said, 'it's everyone else.'

'Oh!' Brian looked up at John, then back at Lauren. 'Isobel says that you and John are going to be married,' he said, his voice hushed. 'She told John she could tell because . . .' He looked at John pleadingly. 'What did she say?'

'She said I looked as if I'd swallowed a bucket of sunshine this morning,' he said, ruffling Brian's hair.

'I guess I'm not always as good at hiding my emotions as I should be. I told Isobel that it wasn't official yet, but that we were going to make plans in that way soon.' He smiled wryly. 'If everything goes as planned,' he added.

'What if it doesn't?' Brian asked, his little face anxious.

Lauren reached over and gave his shoulder a squeeze. 'We'll see that it does,' she said. She handed the coffee-cup back to Brian. 'How about you two gentlemen waiting in the other room while I get dressed?'

John took the cup from Brian and set it on Lauren's nightstand. 'We'll wait in the kitchen,' he said. 'Isobel needs some help baking ginger cookies, and Brian and I are experts.'

What a pair, Lauren thought, watching the two leave the room together. If she could have dreamed the perfect stepfather for Brian, she would not have done as well. She showered and dressed quickly, eager to be with the two men in her life. The sight of Mel Cranston leaning against the kitchen counter and watching with a sour expression on his face while John and Brian rolled out cookies, reminded her that the erstwhile number one man in her life was going to get a very rude shock some day soon. How, she wondered, would he take the news? Badly, she was afraid.

'Good morning, Mel,' she said, trying to sound normal and offhand, in spite of the fact that a rather ominous silence hung over the room. 'How's the law-and-order business these days?'

'So-so,' he replied, a scowl forming over his nose.

'Glad to see you're still talking to me. This place went quiet as a tomb as soon as I walked in. I was wondering what's going on. You any idea?'

Lauren looked pointedly at Mel's somewhat pudgy midsection. 'Maybe they're afraid they'll have to make an extra dozen cookies, now that you're here,' she said.

'Hmmph,' Isobel said, keeping her back to Mel deliberately. 'It doesn't seem to occur to him, when he comes in and the first thing he does is ask John if he doesn't think it would be warmer in Texas this winter, than no one wants to talk to him.'

'Oh, so that's it,' Lauren said, giving Mel a sharp glance. She walked over and stood in front of him. 'Mel, would you please get it through your head that John is not leaving.'

Mel's eyes narrowed. 'He's got to leave some time,' he said.

'No, he doesn't!' Brian said loudly, his tolerance for the conversation apparently exhausted. 'He's gonna stay forever!'

'Hush, Brian,' Lauren said quickly.

'What does he mean, forever?' Mel asked, his round face becoming quite pink.

'He only means that he likes John and doesn't ever want him to leave,' Lauren replied smoothly. 'Now sit down and have some coffee and stop being so grumpy.'

Still glowering, Mel pulled out a chair and sat down. 'Seems to me,' he said pointedly, 'that it's an odd sort of fellow can make a career out of doing odd jobs and poking around asking questions about an old forest fire.'

John, who had been studiously avoiding looking at Mel, handed a tray of cookies to Isobel and then returned his attention to the sheriff. 'Why does it bother you that I'm asking about that?' he enquired.

'It doesn't bother me,' Mel snapped. 'I just think it's a funny thing to do, when there's nothing to know that hasn't already been in the papers. There wasn't any evidence of arson. Me and my deputies had the road sealed off from everything except the fire-fighters as soon as we got the alarm. There wasn't anyone went in or out that we didn't see, and there wasn't anyone there that shouldn't have been there. Not anyone at all.'

'How long after the fire was out would you have seen someone?' John persisted.

'Well, we didn't keep watching for weeks, if that's what you mean,' Mel growled, looking uncomfortable. 'Couldn't have been anyone on that mountain and lived through that fire anyway, unless they were way up above the timber-line. And if there had been anyone up there, we'd have seen their tyre tracks in the ash when they came out.'

Lauren thought she saw a faint flicker of some kind of emotion cross John's face when he heard Mel's denial, but she could not be sure. John definitely had his emotions well controlled at the moment. He merely shrugged.

'I guess that's right,' he said.

'Of course it's right,' Mel said. 'There's nothing more anyone can learn about what happened. So why don't you level with me, Smith, and with Lauren too? Tell us what it is you're really doing here? Who hired you on some kind of wild-goose chase to come up here? I know you aren't some simple country boy, wandering around for no good reason. Lauren already told me how smart you are about business. What is it you're really up to?'

It was Lauren's turn to feel uncomfortable, as John shot her a quick frown. When he almost immediately gave her an amused smile, she explained, 'I got mad at Mel for something he said about you one day, and I happened to mention how you helped with my bookkeeping.'

'That's all right,' John said. 'It doesn't matter now. As to my reason for being here, it's a personal matter, but you'll find out the answer soon enough.'

'Personal matter?' Mel squinted thoughtfully at John. 'Does that mean you've been here before?'

'Could be,' John replied.

'And when you've got this personal matter settled, you're going to be on your way?' Mel asked hopefully.

John glanced at Lauren and then back at Mel. 'No,' he said quietly.

Lauren could almost see the wheels turning in Mel's head as his eyes darted back and forth between her and John. 'I don't think I like what I think is going on,' he said, his face growing pink again. He started to rise from his chair, his voice trembling with rage. 'Lauren, you can't seriously be thinking of marrying this guy, can you?' he shouted, glaring at her.

'Don't yell at me, Mel,' Lauren said warningly. 'Just sit down and keep calm. When there's something definite, you'll be the first to know.'

Instead of sitting, Mel leaped to his feet with such force that he jolted the table and spilled his coffee.

His face was almost purple as he turned towards John. 'If you think you're going to steal her from me, you're crazy!' he said before he stormed out of the room.

'Darn him, anyway!' Lauren cried at the same time as the front door of the lodge could be heard slamming loudly. She blinked back the tears which had sprung to her eyes and sniffed. 'He certainly has a way of spoiling a perfectly beautiful day. I don't like to see him hurt, but . . .'

'But he's brought it on himself,' Isobel interrupted. 'Here.' She handed Lauren a fresh, warm cookie. 'Be a good girl now, and smile. John, give her a hug.'

'Excellent idea,' John agreed.

Lauren smiled, stuffed the cookie into her mouth, and snuggled into John's embrace. 'I guess it's a good day, after all,' she mumbled over the mouthful of spicy cookie. When she had swallowed it, she looked up at John. 'Did you find out anything helpful from Mel?' she asked. 'I thought I saw some kind of a glimmer in your eyes once.'

'I may have,' John replied. 'I think I need to go into the county courthouse and look at some maps of the area. There are still some things that don't jibe with my recollections.'

'Recollections? Then you have been here before?'

'Somewhere near here,' John replied.

Lauren drew her head back and studied John's face. 'You know, I think I'm getting even more curious than Mel is. What kind of a map do you need? I've got a topographical map of the area around here somewhere. We got it when we were first thinking of buying this property.'

'That's the kind I want to look at,' John said

quickly. 'Do you think you can find it?'

'I think it's rolled up in the corner of my closet,' Lauren replied. 'Come on, and I'll look.'

A short time later, they had the map laid out on Lauren's table. 'We're right here,' Lauren said, pointing to the small square on the map that marked the location of the lodge.

John nodded. 'This map is exactly what I needed,' he said. He turned as Brian entered the room. 'What's up, Tiger?' he asked.

'Some people want to check out,' Brian replied. 'I came to get Mommy. Can I see the map, too?'

'Of course,' Lauren said, lifting him up on to a chair. 'I'll go tend to those people. You two find the Holy Grail, or whatever it is you're looking for.'

She had scarcely finished checking the guests out when John and Brian appeared. John's face was grim, but his eyes were so bright with excitement that she knew immediately he had discovered something important on the map. 'Did you find what you were looking for?' she asked.

'I believe so,' he replied. He took a deep breath. 'Can you get away for a few hours? If I can borrow a horse, I'd like you to come with me and verify something. It would be too far to hike, and there isn't any place to drive a car where I want to go.'

'You mean you want me to ride Horse?' Lauren asked apprehensively. She had never taken to riding, especially on an animal that made her feel as if she were a mile from the ground with her feet sticking straight out to the sides.

'If you can sit in a chair you can ride Horse,' John said, amusement at her fears momentarily overcoming the sternness of his features. 'He's the gentlest creature on four feet. Please. It's very important. I'd suggest we ride double, but it might be a little too much for old Horse for a long distance.'

'Well . . . all right,' Lauren agreed. 'I should learn to ride, anyway. The Meltons down the road towards Crook's Crossing have some nice horses. I'll call and see if we can borrow one, and then tell Isobel to take over for me.' Privately, she hoped that the Meltons might not be home or wouldn't loan them a horse, although she could tell from the way John paced back and forth in the hallway while she made her call that his mission was so important that she was going to have to take part in it very soon anyway. When the Meltons were happy to loan them a horse she resigned herself to her fate, and quickly changed into jeans and boots and a warm sweater for the ride.

They rode double on Horse until the reached the Meltons' ranch, then John shortened the stirrups for Lauren and mounted a spirited piebald named Cookie.

'We're going to follow one of the logging roads up the mountain,' John said. 'We won't have to go far on the highway. Just relax and follow me.'

'I'm fine,' Lauren said, trying to smile. Although Horse seemed impervious to the passing traffic, she felt like cringing every time a car passed them.

'Then don't look as if you expect the sky to fall any minute,' John commented drily. 'It's not time for that yet.'

I wonder what he meant by that? Lauren thought. 'Is it going to fall soon?' she called after him.

'Not if I can help it,' he answered cryptically.

Lauren shrugged and concentrated on hanging on tightly to the pommel of her saddle, feeling with every step that she was apt to slide off Horse's broad back and land with a thump on the hard ground. When they turned on to the logging road, John dropped back to ride beside her and give her some riding instructions as they went along.

'But Horse is too fat,' she protested, when John had told her for the third time to keep her knees in and grip Horse with her legs instead of looking like a jumping jack, crouched to leap.

'If he got more exercise he wouldn't be,' John replied. 'But I do think you could use a smaller horse. Cookie here is more your size. Want to try her on the way back?'

Lauren eyed the prancing piebald sceptically. 'I think she'd know right away that I'm a dunce,' she replied. 'I'd better practise for a while on Horse.' She looked around her at the trees. 'It's amazing they were able to keep the fire from coming down here, isn't it? From the highway, you really can't tell there ever was a fire.'

'It was a comparatively small fire, wasn't it?' John said softly. 'Only a couple of hundred acres. I expect that made it harder for you.'

'It did. Sometimes there are thousands of acres afire and hundreds of men fighting the blaze, and no one gets badly hurt. That made me even more angry at the Redferns. They could have handled it without Paul.'

'I'm sure they could have,' John agreed with a grimace. He reined his horse to a stop and pulled a piece of paper from the pocket of his leather jacket. 'I made a sketch from the big map. I think we're about to where the old road goes through,' he said. 'We'll take it back west as far as it goes.'

'As far as it goes?' Lauren looked at him questioningly. 'It goes to the top of the mountain. If you wanted to follow it, we could have driven.'

'No, we couldn't,' John said, shaking his head. 'It stops where the burned area begins now. I want to try to follow where it used to go. Do you think you can remember?'

'I—I should be able to,' Lauren said, trying to swallow the sudden panicky lump in her throat. 'The place where Paul died isn't far from the road. I used to drive up there . . . afterwards.'

'Oh, angel, I'm so sorry,' John said. He reached over and took hold of Lauren's hand. 'I don't want to make you sad, but . . .'

'It's all right,' she said quickly, curling her fingers tightly around John's strong, warm hand. 'It's been a long time. I can't keep running away from my memories forever.'

John looked at her strangely, then raised her hand to his lips and held it there for a long time. 'I know exactly what you mean,' he said at last. 'That's why we're here today. I have some memories to face, too.' He sighed, then smiled briefly. 'Let's go,' he said. He released her hand and clucked to his horse.

In a few minutes they found the crossroad and followed it until, as suddenly as if a time barrier had been passed, the road ended at the edge of a vast area of seedling pines, a new world hidden behind the old.

'For goodness' sake,' Lauren said, looking about her in amazement. 'The road is gone. I wonder why they did that?'

'At least partly for efficiency,' John said drily. 'This timber is well managed. You have to give the Redferns credit for that, anyway.' He pulled out his sketch again and handed it to Lauren. 'Does this help at all?'

Lauren studied the sketch and then looked upwards. 'I think I can find the upper part,' she said. 'Did you want to find the place where it switches back, too?'

'Not necessarily,' John replied. 'I'm most interested in finding the place where it crossed that little creek.'

John's voice had a deep, emotional timbre, in spite of the fact that he spoke quietly. Lauren studied him for a moment, a morbid feeling of impending doom overtaking her at the blank, expressionless face he was now maintaining and the realisation that the spot he wanted to find was only a short distance from the place Paul had fallen. Could there be some terrible connection between him and Paul's death? A shiver of fear went through her. She thought of asking him bluntly, but decided against it. She would, she feared, find out soon enough. 'That shouldn't be hard to find,' Lauren said, biting her lip momentarily before she went on in order to maintain her hard-won composure. 'That creek starts out as a tiny spring, well above the timber-line. I always thought it must come from snow-melt that goes into the ground somewhere. If we can get anywhere near the right spot, I can find that and follow the creek down from there.'

John nodded. 'Lead on,' he said.

Horse plodded stolidly forward. Sitting on his broad, warm back, listening to the creak of the saddle and the sounds of his muffled hoofbeats on the soft red earth, Lauren found herself reliving over and over the times she had come up this mountain admist the blackened stalks of burned trees to stand and stare at the place where her love had died. Tears streamed silently down her cheeks. John saw and stopped his horse.

'Lauren,' he said hoarsely, 'let's not go on. I can't put you through this.'

She shook her head and dashed the tears away angrily. 'I have to do it,' she said. 'Come on.'

She urged Horse forward, keeping her eyes on the farthest reaches of the uphill slope that she could see, angling towards the place where she knew the scrubby growth that signalled the end of the real timber land would appear. When it came in sight, she turned sharply upwards until they reached the very edge of the newly planted pines.

'I'm looking for a certain tree that's a kind of a landmark,' she told John as they began to follow a more horizontal course. 'We should be up high enough to miss that ravine that the road used to dodge around.' It seemed farther than she remembered, but at last an ancient, wind-twisted pine came into view. 'There it is,' she said, pointing. She led John past the tree to a place on the rocky mountainside where several boulders lay close together as if piled there by some giant hand. 'See that little trickle of dampness?' she said, indicating the side of one grey rock. 'That's the very beginning of the creek. It goes underground again and comes out a little farther down as a bit more of a run, but it's still hard to find if you don't know it's there. It wasn't until it got down below the road that it turned into a pretty creek.'

'I must have come up here a dozen times without finding it,' John said, shaking his head sadly. 'I began to think I had either dreamed it or I was in the wrong place after all.' He swung down from his horse and bent to touch the little spring. Lauren dismounted awkwardly and went to stand nearby.

'Do you . . . want to follow the creek downhill?' she asked.

'Might as well try,' John said. He stood up and put his hand on Lauren's shoulder, and looked into her eyes, his own vividly blue and intense. 'No matter what happens later,' he said, 'I want you to know how much it means to me to find this. It answers a question that's been haunting me for a long time.'

'John, can't you tell me . . .' Lauren began. She stopped when John shook his head impatiently.

'Very soon,' he said. He took a deep breath. 'I have to do it in my own way,' he added, giving her a sad little smile. He slid his arm around her shoulders. 'Let's walk along. It may be easier to follow the trickle on foot.'

'All right,' Lauren said, feeling again that ominous cloud, now hanging between them like an unspoken curse. She took Horse's reins and led him along, watching the rocky path for the familiar signs of the increasing flow of the little stream. It was not difficult to follow, but when they reached the edge of the timber land it became impossible. 'They've covered it up!' she cried, pointing to the place where the stream ended. 'They've laid a pipe and covered it up! What an awful thing to do! Is that some more of their blasted efficiency?'

John sighed and squeezed her shoulders. 'I suppose

so,' he said grimly. 'That certainly explains why I couldn't find it down here before.'

'But it was so pretty,' Lauren said, feeling both angry and sad at the same time. She hurried forward, pulling Horse along, pointing ahead of her as she went, ignoring the new trees, remembering in her mind how it had looked before. 'Right about here,' she said a few minutes later, 'is where the road went across. It went on around the mountain and then up out of the timber to some old cabins.' She rushed forward, pell mell, down the steep slope. 'Look over there,' she said. 'Those rocks are from the stream bed. It got bigger here. And down here . . .' she stumbled to a stop, 'there was quite a large pool, with ferns along the banks that were still green after the fire.' She turned, now almost frantic at the remembrance that seemed so vivid, and waved an arm towards the east. 'Over there, only about a hundred feet, is the spot where Paul was found. I used to wonder why he couldn't have found the stream. Why he couldn't have got just that little bit farther. If he had, he might have been safe. They said afterwards that they didn't know why he was over here anyway.' She turned her tear-streaked face to John. 'He wasn't supposed to . . .'

She stopped. John's head was bowed, his eyes closed, and tears were now running down his cheeks. 'John,' she said, her voice hushed at the sight of his sorrow, 'what is it? Were you there? Did you see him?'

John opened his eyes, his expression tortured, as if he, too, were reliving that day. 'I was there,' he said. 'I didn't see him.'

'But what . . .' Lauren began.

'Shhh,' John said, attempting a smile and placing a finger gently against Lauren's lips. He took her into his arms and held her close to him. She could feel the rapid, heavy beating of his heart, the tension that made his body hard as steel against her. 'Let's find the road up to those old cabins,' he murmured against her ear. 'We can rest up there, and I'll tell you everything you want to know. And some things you probably don't.'

CHAPTER NINE

ONCE they were above the timber forest on a more westerly slope of the mountain, the remains of the old road were still visible. Lauren followed John, her nerves so taut that she dared not think what might be in store for her at the end of their ride. One thing was crystal-clear from both what John had said and his obvious anxiety over telling her. Whatever it was was not going to be pleasant. She pushed aside every ugly, frightening image that tried to invade her mind, instead staring at John's broad shoulders as he rode ahead of her, sitting in his saddle easily, his dark head erect, his hair ruffled softly by the cool breeze. She loved him so. Nothing that he could tell her would change that, she vowed. Nothing.

They followed the road until it faded into a dim trail near the top of the mountain, a few yards short of the spot where once two cabins had stood. Only the ramshackle walls of the cabins were still standing, a partial roof giving one of them a rakish air, as if it wore a hat at an extreme angle.

John swung down from his horse and then helped Lauren to dismount. Silently, he took her hand and led her past the cabins to a spot where a huge rock provided a vantage-point across seemingly endless miles of mountain ranges. Row upon row of mountains, each a slightly paler shade of bluish purple, shaded away in a never-ending progression until at last they faded into oneness with the sky and defined the very edge of the visible earth.

'What a magnificent view,' Lauren murmured. 'I'd forgotten how beautiful it is. After Paul died, I used to come up here and sit on this rock and try not to think of anything at all. It always made me feel at peace, looking out across the top of the world like this. It's hard to feel that you and your problems are very earthshaking when you look at those mountains and think how long they've been here.' She felt John's hand tighten around hers and looked up at him. He was looking across the mountain-tops, his expression ineffably sad.

'I'm glad you feel that way, too,' he said softly. 'That makes it a good place to talk.' He put his arm around Lauren and hugged her against him. 'Perhaps some day we ought to build a cabin up here, with a huge stone fireplace and windows that look out across the mountains, where we could come to be alone and feel at peace with the world.'

'That's a . . . lovely idea,' Lauren said wistfully, thinking longingly of the image John's words created, 'but something like that would be terribly expensive. Not to mention the fact that the Redfern Timber Company owns all of this land, too.' She looked up at John and frowned. 'Besides, I don't think that's what we came here to talk about.'

'In a way, it is,' John said. He pulled Lauren even tighter against him for a moment and dropped a kiss on her hair. 'Let's sit down,' he said. 'I don't think either one of us can take this standing up.' He sat down, cross-legged, and waited until Lauren had done the same. 'The Redfern Timber Company does own this,' he said then, looking first around him at the vast scene before them and then back at Lauren, 'but that presents no problem.' He paused and looked at her with such intensity that Lauren felt as if he were trying to get his next words into her mind without actually saying them. A moment later, she knew why. 'I'm Jonathan Redfern,' he said.

For what seemed like an eternity, Lauren stared at him, speechless, his words echoing in her ears. John had told her something very startling, but somehow it did not seem to make anything happen inside her. He was still the same man he had been only a few moments ago, wasn't he? 'Jonathan Redfern?' she said finally, in a tiny voice. 'The one who disappeared?'

John nodded. 'Yes,' he said. 'The one who disappeared.'

Lauren blinked, trying to comprehend what that might mean, but feeling nothing so much as a whirling confusion. 'I don't understand,' she said, feeling panicky at her inability to make any sense of what John had said. 'Are you trying to tell me that John Smith doesn't exist? That you're really someone else? Why did you pretend to be someone named John Smith? What are you hiding from?'

'Nothing, really, any more,' John said. He reached over and took Lauren's hands in his. 'Before I tell you the whole story,' he said, 'I want you to understand one thing. This is very important, Lauren. John Smith is perfectly real. I have never pretended to be a different person from the one I am. I am still exactly the same man you know as John Smith. In fact, I intend to keep that name from now on. There's no point in trying to go back to something that never really fitted me, anyway, although it took me a long time to learn that it didn't.' He smiled gently and tightened his hands around Lauren's. 'I hope you don't hate me because I'm one of those horrible Redferns?'

'Hate you, John?' Lauren said hoarsely, tears clouding her vision as she studied the dear face before her, with its strong angles and deep lines, the eyes so blue that they seemed to have brought a piece of the sky down from heaven. She could see him waiting now, watching from behind that vivid blue, his whole heart exposed, wondering if she would run from what he had told her, despising him for being born with a name that was not the one she knew. But she didn't. That was something for her mind. Nothing in her heart had changed. Her mind still needed to know why he had disappeared, taken another name, and then come back to find some lost memories near the spot where Paul had died, but first she must tell him what was in her heart.

'Of course I don't hate you,' she said softly. 'I still love you just the same.' She could see the terrible tension evaporate from John's face in a flash, replaced by a smile so radiant that it made her feel dizzy with answering joy. She moved into his outstretched arms, seeking their warmth with a relief that sent the last clouds of fear flying.

'My wonderful, heavenly angel,' he murmured, showering her face with little kisses. 'How strong you are. How beautiful, how dear. Do you know, I lay awake most of last night just watching you and loving you, for fear that if I went to sleep my dreams would all be of my telling you my other name and you running away from me? I'm ashamed of myself now. I should have had more confidence in you.'

'Yes, you should,' Lauren replied, nuzzling his ear affectionately. 'A rose by any other name, and all that.'

'No one ever accused me of being a rose,' John said drily, 'except for the thorns.' He shifted Lauren so that he could look into her face. 'Do you mind if I hold you while I tell you the rest?' he asked. 'I promise I'll let go if you decide I'm too bad a character for you, after all.'

'I won't,' Lauren said positively. 'I think I'm ready for almost anything.'

'All right,' John said. 'Hang on. You won't think much of the Redfern name when I'm through. Do you remember what I told you about Jenny?' When Lauren nodded, he went on. 'Well, when I first discovered her with my stepbrother, Kevin, I blamed him for seducing an innocent. I vowed to get revenge, one way or another. For years he'd been flaunting his money, always seeming to have far more to spend than I did. He worked in the home offices of Redfern Industries. I worked in the construction department. That's how I came to know how to do all kinds of jobs, since my father insisted I work my way up, starting when I was only in high school. Later, though, after I graduated from college, I was in the management end. I wasn't really connected with the main office, which runs the timber business, but I began to wonder if there might not be something interesting going on with Kevin's accounts. I looked into it, on the sly, and discovered that he had been pulling all kinds of illegal tricks with my father's money. Not only that, but he had some dealings with the underworld that looked very suspicious.

'I gathered quite a bit of information, ready to spring it all on my father. Over the years, my stepmother had managed to drive a wedge between us. She wanted everything for her precious Kevin, and my father, who needed a strong woman to lean on after my mother died, never did seem to realise what she was doing. I thought I had found the perfect way to get my revenge, although now . . .' John paused and sighed, 'I think that was a stupid idea. It would only have made my father unhappy. Anyway, one night Kevin appeared at my door with a bottle in his hand, suggesting that we bury the hatchet over a drink or two. That was, I believe, the night before the fire here.'

John paused for a breath, and Lauren asked, 'That was in San Francisco?'

'That's right,' John said. 'I invited him in, not even slightly interested in forgiving him, but very interested in what he would say when I told him what I had found out. I never got a chance. My guess is that somehow he discovered what I'd been up to. Anyway, I took the drink he handed me, had a swallow or two, and that is the last thing I remember until . . .' John shuddered involuntarily and his arms tightened around Lauren '. . . a feeling that I was choking to death. I opened my eyes. There was smoke all around me and the roar of a fire. I looked up and a wall of fire was coming towards me.' John paused again and Lauren clung to him silently, remembering with him the horror that she had imagined so often. Then he went on, in a deep, intense voice, 'I remember screaming and trying to get up. All I could manage was a kind of half crawl. I went away from the flames as fast as I could, and, by the grace of God, fell into that creek, at what must have been the deep little pool you remember. I lay there for what seemed like forever, huddled in the pool, trying to stay beneath the water, trying not to breathe. Finally, the flames passed by. I crawled up the creek until I got to the place where no fire had been. Then I just lay there for a long time. I could tell that my nose was broken, some of my ribs, and I had a huge lump on my head. Apparently, after I had fallen unconscious from some kind of drug, Kevin, or someone he had with him, had beaten me for good measure. I couldn't remember who I was, what had happened before the fire, or how in hell I happened to be there. After dark, I managed to get on my feet. There was a moon, so I could see fairly well. I went on up the mountain, down the other side, and hitched a ride to Texas. When the trucker asked the name of the awful-looking derelict he'd picked up, I told him John Smith. It was the only name I could think of, and there was nothing in my pockets to tell me otherwise. For a long time I didn't remember, but finally it started coming back and I knew that somehow dear Kevin had left me there to die in a fire he may well have set, although I don't think there's any way to prove that now. I used to think that what happened to me was the worst part of the fire, but now I know it wasn't.' John looked into Lauren's eyes, his own eyes misted and sad. 'It's possible that Paul saw me or heard me scream and came looking for me. I may be responsible for his death.'

Lauren shook her head and reached up to lay her hand alongside his cheek. 'No, John,' she said. 'It's Kevin who's responsible if he did. He put you there. Don't blame yourself. I certainly couldn't. And if Kevin started the fire, he's responsible whether Paul saw you or not.'

'I suppose that's true,' John said with a heavy sigh. 'Of course, I still have no memory for the period between taking that drink and waking up to see the fire. I wouldn't have believed Kevin brought me here himself, and I still think he may have had help, except that I found something under the old floorboards in the first cabin behind us when I came up here to look around one day.' He pulled a large pocket knife from his pocket. Engraved on it were the initials K.R. 'Dad gave Kevin this knife when he was fourteen,' John said, holding it out for Lauren to see. 'He never went anywhere without it.'

'A Swiss army knife?' Lauren asked, turning it over in her hand. She smiled when John nodded. 'I used to want one of those. I suppose Brian will, too, some time.' She handed the knife back to John. 'I still don't understand why you came back here, if you remembered most of what happened. Why didn't you go back to San Francisco and file some charges against Kevin?'

'I wanted to check out the details,' John replied. 'I was still pretty fuzzy on what happened those first few hours after I regained consciousness. It seemed to me that if I wanted any charges to stick, especially after being away for a couple of years, I'd better have my facts straight.'

'Did it take you two years to remember who you

really were?' Lauren asked.

'No, only a couple of months,' John answered, grimacing. 'It took me two years to decide what I wanted to do about the whole thing. I was enjoying life on that ranch. It seemed stupid to give that up, and go back to a place with such wretched memories. I didn't care about revenge, or bringing Kevin to justice, or whatever you want to call it. I knew my father would miss me, but I was afraid that finding out the truth about Kevin would be too much for him. He's not a strong man. And yet, I couldn't see myself going back and acting as if nothing had happened except that I'd had a lapse of memory and gone away for a while. All in all, Texas seemed a better place to be. But, when the rancher sold out, I decided to come back just long enough to straighten things out and get old Kevin under lock and key. I was going to head back to Texas as soon as I could. Then the strangest thing happened.'

John looked down at Lauren and smiled, a warm, happy light again in his beautiful eyes. 'I met this adorable little golden-haired angel on the highway, and from then on I never thought of Texas again, until . . .' he made a wry face, 'until I got scared that she didn't really love me, or at least didn't care enough to be able to handle what I've told her today. I still can't quite believe that you've heard it all without a quiver. Are you sure you aren't just waiting to bolt and run away?'

'You try and get rid of me and see what happens,' Lauren said, smiling and rising on to her knees to kiss John firmly on the mouth. She locked her arms behind his neck and tilted her head to one side. 'Tell me, my love,' she said, 'what are you going to do now that you do have all the details you need? Are you going to finally let Mel in on it so that he can help bring the villain to justice?'

John's expression clouded again. 'I'm afraid not,' he said. 'There's some chance he may have seen Kevin leaving here after the fire. I believe that Kevin, probably with an accomplice because I doubt he's strong enough to have carried my dead weight, must have deposited me down below the timber-line. Then they either started the fire, or had the good luck of nature starting one. After that, they came to these old cabins to wait it out. You know how fast a fire goes when it's dry. Once it was going well enough for them to be sure it was going to do the job, they could never have driven out through it. When it was over, they drove out leaving, as Mel said, a nice trail through the ashes.'

'You mean,' Lauren said, frowning, 'that you think Mel saw Kevin and didn't report it?'

'I don't know,' John replied, tracing the edge of her cheeks with his fingertips, his brows drawn together in a worried crease. 'I know Kevin would happily have bribed him if he did. I hate to think it of Mel, because I know he's an old friend of yours even though he's an irritant, too. But why else would he mention tyre tracks in the ashes? Tell me, Lauren, do you think Mel could be bought, or is he as honest and upright as he seems?'

'Oh, I'm almost positive that he's completely honest,' Lauren replied quickly. 'Isn't it possible that even if he saw Kevin, he'd think it was perfectly all right for a Redfern to be here? Maybe you could just ask him if he saw Kevin.'

'I wish I could,' John said, frowning, 'but if there's any chance he might have taken a bribe, I'd rather not. He might let Kevin know someone was asking, and I'd like to keep the element of surprise on my side. I wouldn't want Kevin to get suspicious and decide to leave the country. I'll just go on in to San Francisco next week and get the legal wheels in motion. The sooner it's all over with, the sooner the two of us can settle down to a nice, quiet life together at the lodge, with only a few dozen guests to cope with at a time, and all of the pleasures of this beautiful country to enjoy. In case you wondered, I have no intention of going back to Redfern Industries. I'll take what's mine, including this mountaintop, and bid them a not very fond farewell.' He got up and helped Lauren to her feet. 'How can I ever tell you,' he asked, taking her into his arms, 'how very grateful I am to you for understanding everything today? For coming into my life? For being the most wonderful woman in the world?'

Lauren made a face at him. 'You'd better stop flattering me like that. I might begin to believe it. And if you're looking for some way to tell me, why don't you stop talking and kiss me? It seems like forever since I had a real kiss from you.'

'Then believe that everything I said is true,' John said, lowering his mouth to hers.

The passion of John's kiss was so intense that Lauren felt at first as if she had actually begun to fly above the mountaintops, the breeze swirling around her in rainbow mists that made a cocoon around them in their own special world. Her lips parted to John's devouring longing, her arms holding him close, wanting nothing so much as to make him a part of her, so that he would never again doubt the strength of her love. When at last he raised his head she clung to him, not wanting the moment to end, leaning her head against his chest, her eyes closed.

'Believe always that I love you, John,' she said huskily.

'I will,' he replied, lowering his head to rest his cheek against her hair. He rested it there for a moment and then sighed. 'I expect we'd better start for home,' he said. 'We don't want anyone to worry.'

'I suppose so,' Lauren agreed. She took one last look out across the mountaintops. 'Can we really have a cabin here?' she asked. 'Will they let you have this mountaintop?'

'They owe me a lot. I can easily have the whole damned mountain,' John replied. 'In fact, I think I may demand it.' He chuckled at Lauren's surprised expression. 'I don't think it's quite sunk in with you yet, but I have quite a large fortune of my own. There will be no more worries about paying the mortgage off.'

'I guess that doesn't seem quite real yet,' Lauren said, as John helped her back into Horse's saddle.

'You'll get used to it,' John said, swinging easily on to his horse. 'I wanted to tell you that a long time ago, but there was no way I could. Besides, it was more of a challenge to see if we could make the lodge pay its own way. Almost too much of one.'

'I know,' Lauren said, 'but I don't want things to change too much. I don't want to find myself sitting around with nothing to do.'

'My love,' John said, looking over at her and smiling, 'that will never happen. You will still run the lodge, I will still do all of the repairs, and when we build our cabin, I intend to do most of the work myself. Money's nice to have, but only if you use it to do what you want to do, not if you let it run your life and make you do things or buy things to impress other people.'

'I should have known you'd feel that way, shouldn't I?' Lauren said, feeling a little embarrassed.

'Yes, ma'am, I think you should have,' John replied in his best Texas drawl.

As they started back down the mountain, John said, 'I don't think we'd better mention anything about all of this to anyone yet. I definitely don't want Mel to hear about it before I've gone to San Francisco. For your sake, I hope he's not involved, but if he is . . .'

'It could ruin his career in law enforcement, couldn't it?' Lauren finished for him.

'I'm afraid so,' John said sadly. He was thoughtfully silent for a few minutes, then he turned towards Lauren and said, 'What do you say we forget about the whole damned mess for the rest of today? Instead, let's decide how many more children we're going to have. I was thinking we might have a dozen, and just take over the lodge-rooms for them, one by one.'

'A dozen?' Lauren squeaked. 'Now *that* would be the mess to end all messes! If I had a dozen children, I'd spend most of my time in that cabin on the mountain, trying to hang on to my sanity. How about a brother for Brian and two little girls to keep each other company?'

'That sounds good,' John replied. He suddenly

smiled radiantly at Lauren. 'Hell, that sounds wonderful! I can't believe the future looks so bright for me now, when only yesterday I was the gloomiest man on the face of the earth. I was an idiot to ever think of leaving you. How can you ever consider marrying such an idiot?'

'Because I'm an idiot, too, I guess,' Lauren replied with a sigh. 'If I'd only told you I loved you sooner, you'd never have thought of leaving. I do hope all of our children won't be idiots. Do you suppose it's hereditary?'

'Not likely.' John's expression became thoughtful again. 'I think, though, that we'll have to be sure to teach them to talk about their fears instead of hiding them inside and pretending that everything is fine. Even when I sounded as though I had life all figured out, I would often lie awake at night and wonder if it wasn't all too good to last.'

'I know how that feels,' Lauren said soberly. 'You wonder if you dare to be really happy, for fear it may all be taken away from you again.' She gave John a rueful smile. 'I might as well admit that I'm still a little scared.'

'So am I,' John replied. 'I think only time will make it go away completely.' He looked back at Horse and then reined his piebald to a halt. 'Looks as if your trusty steed has a sore foot,' he said. 'We'd better stop for a minute.' He swung down and examined Horse's rear left hoof. 'Poor guy's got a rock caught in his hoof,' he said. 'I'm going to need a hoof-pick to get it out.' He stood up and held out his arms towards Lauren. 'I think you'd better ride with me the rest of the way. I must admit I'm not too sorry old Horse gave me an excuse to have you do that.'

'Neither am I,' Lauren said, eagerly sliding off Horse's broad back and into John's waiting arms. Instantly she found herself in another passionate embrace. This time, John did not stop kissing her until she was gasping for breath, her head spinning so dizzily that she was sure she could not have ridden alone again if she had wanted to. 'Stop it, John,' she breathed, trying unsuccessfully to pull herself free. The currents of desire that were surging through her were almost maddening.

'I don't want to stop,' he growled, pulling her down on the soft pine-needle mat beneath the trees. He flung one leg across her, one hand pressing her against his undulating hips, the other hand behind her neck, holding her head captive for his devouring mouth. His breathing was ragged. 'Oh, lord, Lauren, I want you so,' he groaned. 'I love you so.' He clutched her to him and rolled completely over once, and then again. To Lauren it felt as if she were caught in a maelstrom of sensations that were so overwhelming that all she could do was to hang on and weather the storm, hoping for some relief from the waves of longing that threatened to overwhelm her. Her legs tightened around John's, so that they rolled as one down the slope until they came to rest with a thump against a tree. The jolt sent a series of spasms so strong that they radiated through Lauren, curling her toes. She caught her breath repeatedly, clinging tightly to John, at first unable to believe what had happened. John took one last deep, shuddering breath, and then lay still, his eyes closed, breathing heavily. A few moments later he raised his head, a little smile quirking the corners of his mouth, his eyes full of laughing lights.

'That's the first time I've pulled a stunt like that since I was in high school,' he said. 'It's not the most rewarding experience in the world. I'm sorry. You must think I'm a regular animal.

Lauren tried to look severe, but failed, instead bursting out laughing. 'I guess I'm one too,' she said.

For a moment John looked startled, then he, too, began to laugh. Together they laughed and rolled back and forth on the piney carpet until they were both gasping for breath. At last, John jumped to his feet and helped Lauren up.

'What a woman,' he said, attempting to brush the pine needles from Lauren's hair and sweater.

'I think I'm going to need a comb for this mess,' Lauren said, feeling the needles embedded in her hair. 'Here, let me brush you off.' She removed the debris from John's broad back, then began to work her way down. Suddenly she stopped, then giggled. John looked over his shoulder at her, one eyebrow raised questioningly. 'I was just thinking what fun it is to be able to do this,' she said, slowly and carefully flicking her hand across his slim hips and buttocks.

John chuckled. 'Can't say that I mind it, either,' he replied, 'but I'll like it even better when you can soap me in the shower.'

Lauren stopped her brushing and straightened. 'That will be fun, won't it?' she said. She threw her arms around John's chest and hugged him, her heart suddenly bursting with a new kind of warm happiness. 'I can hardly wait,' she said, looking up at him and smiling. 'There are so many wonderful things that we can do together . . . I can hardly believe it's only going to be a little while before we can.'

'Believe it,' John said, his voice deep and soft, his eyes alight with love. 'It will only be a little while longer.'

They rode back to the lodge, talking happily about their plans for the future. John suggested adding a building behind the lodge that could be used for meetings. 'Then we might get some small church conferences and such,' he said.

'That's a great idea!' Lauren said enthusiastically. 'We're going to need to add on to our apartment, too,' she added.

'Or build a separate house,' John said. 'Which would you prefer?'

'I don't know,' Lauren replied. 'We'll have to think about that for a while.'

They stopped at the Meltons' and borrowed a hoof-pick, so that John could alleviate Horse's suffering, then rode the patient old horse back to the lodge. John's breath was soft and warm against Lauren's cheek as he helped her down, then held her tightly again, seeming never to want her far from him.

She sighed and raised her head to touch his chin with her lips. 'I'll be so glad when we're married,' she said. 'I still feel as if I'm living in a dream, a little afraid that I may wake up and discover that was all it was.'

'You won't,' John said softly. 'And even if I have to move mountains, I'm going to see that all of your dreams come true.'

Lauren reminded John of that statement the next morning when he was helping her to carry what seemed like an endless number of bags of groceries from the jeep to the kitchen.

'We're going to have to have more storage so I don't have to shop so often,' she complained. 'I think we need another freezer and refrigerator.'

'And a bigger pantry,' Isobel added.

'Yes, ma'am,' John agreed. 'We can probably get some wholesalers to deliver directly to us by next spring. Maybe even sooner. I'll look into that.'

'John's a mighty smart fellow,' Isobel commented to Lauren when he had gone to retrieve more of the groceries. 'I've always wondered how he happened to be hitch-hiking that day you had your flat tyre. Has he ever told you?'

'No. Not . . . not exactly,' Lauren replied, wishing that she did not have to continue the deception. It gave her a strange feeling, as if the real world was not the one she was living in.

Isobel shrugged. 'Oh, well, maybe it's something we wouldn't really want to know.'

'Why do you say that?' Lauren asked sharply, wondering if Mel had been around again, spreading his ridiculous ideas.

'I'm not sure,' Isobel replied. She shook her head. 'I guess I've listened to too much of Mel's foolishness. That man's always hearing footsteps behind him. Oh, by the way . . .' Isobel stopped unloading groceries and looked over at Lauren, 'Mel's new deputy stopped by for coffee this morning. Nice young man. His name's Keith Wellington. He said Mel's Aunt Tillie is in the hospital in San Francisco. Mel's gone to visit her. She's in pretty bad shape, so he said.'

Lauren felt as if an electric shock had gone through

her from her head to her toes. 'He's in San Francisco?' she asked sharply.

'That's what Keith said,' Isobel replied. 'Why? Do you know his aunt?'

'Oh . . . no,' Lauren said, shaking her head. 'That's too bad, isn't it?'

'What's too bad?' John asked, coming into the room and depositing his bags of groceries on the counter.

'Mel's gone to San Francisco to see his Aunt Tillie,' Lauren replied, giving John a meaningful look. 'She's . . . in the hospital.'

'Sorry to hear that,' John said smoothly, although his expression became grim and he motioned for Lauren to follow him back outside. 'Does Mel often visit this Aunt Tillie?' he asked.

'It's the first time I ever heard of her,' Lauren replied. 'Do you suppose he went all the way there to see Kevin?'

John shook his head. 'I don't know why he'd do that. Is there some way we could find out if Mel really has an Aunt Tillie in the hospital?'

Lauren bit her lip thoughtfully. 'I could call his office and see if they know which hospital she's in,' she said. 'If they know that, I could call and ask to talk to her.'

John nodded. 'Good idea. Do that, would you please, while I get the last of the groceries?'

When John joined Lauren in her apartment a few minutes later, she shook her head. 'No one knows anything about Mel's Aunt Tillie,' she said. 'He left at about noon yesterday and said he wasn't sure when he would be back, but that it would be as soon as possible.' She studied John's worried frown. 'What's wrong, John?' she asked.

'I suddenly realised what may have happened to that saw I've been using,' John replied. 'Mel may have taken it to get a set of fingerprints. He may know who I am. I don't know why I didn't think of that sooner, or why he didn't do it sooner, as hostile as he's been.'

Lauren's heart sank. 'Probably because I threatened never to speak to him again if he did,' she said in a low voice. 'He wanted to do that once, a long time ago. But would they have them on file? You're not a criminal.'

'They'd have them,' John replied. 'I've had a security check.' He sighed heavily. 'I'm still not really sure what Mel would hope to gain by going to see Kevin, unless after he discovered what my other name is he figured the whole thing out and planned to try a little extortion. I doubt that. Mel's not that sharp.' He frowned, and then shrugged. 'Mel's probably not involved at all. I'm just getting anxious now that it's time to end the waiting. I think I'll go to San Francisco in the morning, myself, as soon as Brian and I get back from the fishing expedition I promised him. the sooner I do that, the sooner we can be married and live happily ever after.'

'I'll vote for that,' Lauren said, melting against John as he put his arms around her. 'I'm getting nervous, too. I think it's still that fear that something will go wrong, don't you?'

'I'm afraid so,' John said with a sigh. 'All the more reason to get moving, before our nerves have to take any more of a beating. I want everything in your life to be absolutely perfect from now on.'

'I want that for you, too,' Lauren said, lifting her face for a kiss, and feeling a brief but warm happiness as John complied. 'I do wish I could go with you tomorrow,' she said. 'I'm going to be worried the whole time you're gone.'

'There's nothing to worry about,' John said, kissing her again. 'I wish you could go, too, but it wouldn't be a good idea this time. We'll go to San Francisco together some time soon, I promise. Maybe even for our honeymoon. Would you like that?'

'I'd love it,' Lauren said. 'It's my favourite city. But don't you think it's a little soon to talk of our honeymoon? After all, we're not officially engaged yet.'

John's eyes twinkled with mischief. 'Don't get smart with me, woman,' he said. 'You're mine, and you know it. I think what you need is some serious kissing.' With that, he lowered his mouth to find Lauren's with a long, passionate kiss that swept away the anxieties that talk of his trip had produced, and left her with that wonderful feeling of elation that only the touch of his lips could produce. But the feeling faded quickly, and for the rest of the day she suffered from a gnawing feeling of dread that no amount of common sense could seem to erase.

'I wish you didn't have to go tomorrow,' she said, caressing John's cheek when he came to kiss her goodnight. 'I don't know why, but it scares me. Couldn't it be dangerous, confronting Kevin? After all, if he tried to kill you once . . .'

'Nothing I can't handle,' John replied. He smiled gently at Lauren's worried frown. 'I'll be all right, angel,' he said. 'Don't worry.' When Lauren's eyes filled with tears, he swore softly. 'I suppose that's what Paul told you, too, isn't it?' he asked.

'Almost exactly,' she said hoarsely.

John threw back Lauren's covers and slid in beside her. 'I'm sleeping with you tonight,' he said firmly. 'I can't have you crying yourself to sleep all alone in here while I'm out on the sofa. It's time you got used to the idea that I'm going to be with you, come hell or high water, for the rest of your life.' He took her in his arms, and cradled her against his shoulder until she fell asleep.

Lauren awoke when John got up early to take Brian fishing, smiling contendedly as he kissed her goodbye. It had been a blissful night, waking from time to time to find herself still held close to John, his warmth comforting and solid. She loved the way he felt, his slender body firm to her touch, his long legs curved around her like a protective shield, his arm tucked across her to keep her safe. More than once she had thought how easy it would be to arouse him, to tease him into making love, but she had restrained herself, knowing how seriously he had meant that he wanted to wait. He was right, of course, but how she longed for the next few days to pass. She sighed and turned over, trying to let herself drift off to sleep again. It was no use. Without John's arms around her, the anxiety returned. She might as well get up and face the day. It was only a little past eight when John and Brian returned, Brian excitedly exhibiting a nice trout that he had caught.

'Should I fix it for your breakfast?' Lauren asked him.

Brian nodded. 'Boy, was that a hard one to catch,'

he said. 'He fought and fought. And John didn't hardly help me at all.'

'I didn't,' John confirmed with a grin when Lauren shot him a sceptical look. 'Hardly at all.'

The telephone on the kitchen wall rang, and Isobel answered it. A moment later she held the phone out towards John. 'It's for you,' she said. 'That new deputy.'

John took the phone from her. 'Hello?' He listened intently for a few minutes, frowning more deeply by the moment. 'All right,' he said at last, 'I'll be there right away.' He turned to Lauren and grimaced. 'I guess my trip will have to wait for a couple of hours while I do my civic duty. It seems a rogue bear attacked a Mrs McCutcheon this morning in Crook's Creek while she was hanging out her washing. They're getting a posse together to track it down and shoot it with a tranquilliser so it can be examined. I'll be back as soon as I can.'

'Oh, dear,' Lauren said, biting her lip. 'Do be careful. Where are you meeting?'

'In front of the post office,' John replied, bending to give her a quick kiss. 'You'd better warn the guests not to go hiking in the woods until we catch the critter. You can never tell which direction it might decide to go, and they can cover ground pretty fast.'

'I wish I could go,' Brian said wistfully.

John crouched before him. 'When you're a little bigger, Tiger,' he said, 'we'll go hunting and fishing all over these mountains. Today, you'd better stay close and help your mother so she doesn't have to worry about you, too. OK?'

'OK,' Brian agreed, smiling as John hugged him.

'You be careful, 'cause bears can be real fierce.'

'You bet,' John said. 'I'll be the most careful man in those woods.' He picked up his hat, and hurried out of the door.

Lauren watched him go, a knot that felt as big as a grapefruit forming in her midsection. Then she sighed heavily and shook her head. Would she never get over this terrible fear? It wasn't as if John was going off to war, or even going to search for the bear alone. There would be a lot of other men there. He would be perfectly safe.

CHAPTER TEN

IN SPITE of Lauren's continual admonitions to herself to be calm, the morning dragged by more slowly than any morning she could remember, the gnawing feeling that something was wrong impossible to shake. Had she been mistaken, after all, in declaring her love for John? Was it going to be impossible for her to deal with her fears? She had better make up her mind, for John was not going to stay home with her all of the time in order to keep her from worrying. Her mind flip-flopped from one point of view to the other, while she kept an anxious eye on the clock.

Nancy had had to go to the dentist that morning, and had told Lauren she should be at work by ten o'clock. By the time that Nancy arrived, Lauren felt as if every nerve in her body was ready to fracture from sheer tension. 'Has anyone seen the bear yet?' Lauren demanded, intercepting her on the porch of the lodge.

'Bear?' Nancy looked puzzled. 'What bear?'

Lauren felt her heart begin to pound. Something *was* wrong. Very wrong. 'The . . . the rogue bear that attacked Mrs McCutcheon in Crook's Creek this morning,' she said, her voice barely audible.

Nancy looked at Lauren curiously. 'Are you sure you got the story right?' she asked. 'I saw Mrs McCutcheon in Briggsville a little while ago. She didn't say anything about a bear.'

A cold sweat broke out all over Lauren's trembling

body. She was sure she had heard the name correctly, but suddenly she knew what she had not heard—the sound of an ambulance screaming by on the highway, carrying the victim from Crook's Creek to the hospital in Briggsville. 'Dear lord,' Lauren murmured. Either her imagination was running away with her, or someone had lured John to Crook's Creek with that story about a rogue bear. Mel's deputy had called, but could Mel have told him to? Could Mel be in league with Kevin Redfern, about to try to accomplish what Kevin had failed to do two years before? If he was . . .

A white-hot anger surged through Lauren, erasing her fear and mobilising her with a determination to find out the truth no matter what the cost. 'Nancy,' she said, 'may I borrow your car?'

'Of course,' Nancy replied. 'Where are you going?'

'I'm not sure. Tell Isobel and Brian I forgot something I needed at the store. And keep a very close eye on Brian, will you? He knows I've been worried about John. I don't want him to be worried, too.'

Without waiting for a reply, Lauren took the porch steps in one leap and raced to Nancy's little car. At the highway she paused, then turned towards Crook's Creek. She had first better verify the truth of falsity of the bear story with some of the local people. In less than ten minutes she was hurrying into the general store, where all of the current gossip was passed between the residents. If anything as unusual as a bear attack had occurred, the air would be filled with it.

Lauren picked up a large box of detergent and carried it to the checkout counter. 'What's new and exciting in Crook's Creek, Tom?' she asked the clerk casually, although her heart pounded as she waited for the answer.

The young man snorted. 'New and exciting? You've gotta be kidding, Mrs Stanley,' he said.

'No desperate criminals walking the streets? No wild animals attacking innocent old ladies?' Lauren persisted, unsure of the young man's criterion for exciting events.

'Not hardly,' the clerk replied as he made change. 'The thrill of the day so far was Mel Cranston talking to some guys in the alley behind the post office early this morning. Someone said one of the men was Kevin Redfern, and he had a fancy red sports car. Anyway, all they did was stand around for a while, and then drive off like their tail was on fire. Hey, you forgot your change!'

'Keep it!' Lauren called back over her shoulder. She threw the box of detergent into the car, got in, and sped off along the mountainous highway to the county sheriff's office in Briggsville as fast as she could safely go. Where had John gone? What had they done to him? Mel Cranston was going to answer some questions, and he was going to answer them truthfully, or one way or another she was going to make him very sorry he hadn't.

Lauren was relieved to see Mel's patrol car parked in front of the little square county office building on the main street of Briggsville. Thank goodness she wasn't going to have to track him down! She ran up the walk and flung the door open to his office.

'All right, Mel Cranston,' Lauren growled, advancing towards him with her hands clenched, 'where is he? I know there wasn't any bear hunt. I know Kevin Redfern was in Crook's Creek this morning. What's happened to John? You'd better tell me, or so help me I'll personally see to it that you never wear that badge again!' The guilty look that came over Mel's face told her immediately that he knew something she should know.

'I—I don't know,' Mel stammered. 'He never showed up.' He stood up and moved around his desk to face Lauren. 'Lauren, there's something I've got to tell you about John Smith,' he began, perspiring visibly. 'He's not . . .'

'If you mean he's really Jonathan Redfern, save it!' Lauren snapped. 'I already know that. I already know a lot of things, Mel Cranston. Now, how about telling me exactly what you've been up to?'

Mel took out a handkerchief and mopped his face. 'I don't know what you mean, Lauren,' he said, his eyes shifting wildly around the room. 'All I wanted to do was collect the reward. Honest. I took some fingerprints and found out who Smith really is. I admit I was hoping I'd find out he was . . . a wanted man. But all I found out was that Kevin Redfern had put up a big reward for all information about his missing brother, so after I saw my Aunt Tillie the other day I went to see him. He was so surprised, I thought he was going to faint. Then he said he wanted to surprise his brother, and that if I'd arrange for them to meet without John knowing Kevin was going to be there, he'd bring the money. I thought it was a funny idea at the time, but rich folks are kind of peculiar so I agreed to do it. Then this morning . . .' Mel stopped, looking thoroughly miserable.

'This morning what?' Lauren shouted.

'Nothing, really,' Mel said, shaking his head, 'except I recognised the guy Redfern had with him. He's a mobster from San Francisco with a bad reputation. All of a sudden, I wasn't too sure they planned a real warm welcome for John Smith. I was awfully glad he didn't show up. I really was.' He looked pleadingly at Lauren. 'I didn't mean any harm, and John must have got suspicious, so I expect he's all right. Hasn't he come back to the lodge?'

'No,' Lauren replied. She bit her lip. Could she trust Mel's story? It sounded straightforward enough, and gelled with the little she'd heard in Crook's Creek. Assuming it was true, where would John have gone if he had suspected something? What could have made him suspicious? Perhaps she had better trust Mel and see what he could deduce. 'Mel,' she said, 'I want you to listen very closely.' As briefly as she could, Lauren outlined the story John had told her of Kevin's attempt on his life, including that fact that John had wondered if Mel had seen Kevin later. When she had finished, Mel's face was a ghostly grey. 'What is it, Mel,' she demanded. 'Did you see Kevin Redfern?'

Mel nodded, rubbing his hand across his forehead repeatedly. 'I saw Kevin Redfern on the highway the next day after the fire. He was driving one of those four-wheeler deals. A Bronco, I think. It was all sooty, and so was he. Said he'd been inspecting the damage, but not to tell anyone because his old man would be mad at him for going in there so soon. I didn't think anything of it, so I said OK.'

'Did he offer you a bribe not to tell?' Lauren asked.

'Yeah, but I didn't take it,' Mel replied, looking

offended. 'I told him my word was good. And I never said anything about that when I went to see him. I didn't have any idea there was a connection, and Kevin sure didn't let on that there was. He must have put up that reward so no one would ever suspect anything.'

'I expect so,' Lauren said slowly, frowning. 'Where do you suppose John went? How could he have guessed something was wrong?'

Mel took a deep breath and scratched his head. 'He might have seen Bob Melton. Bob was out riding this morning when I went by. John would probably have thought Bob would be one of the people we'd call to go after a bear, and if he saw him he might have stopped to see if he wanted a ride.'

'Call him and see,' Lauren demanded.

A few minutes later, Mel had confirmed his hypothesis. 'Bob says as soon as John found out he hadn't heard of any bear hunt he turned around and headed the other way like a bat out of hell. From what you said, I'd guess that he'd figure either I was setting him up to trap him, or for Kevin to do it. He'd want to get to San Francisco first and surprise that ugly stepbrother of his at the other end. He'd have had a good hour's head start.'

'In that jeep?' Lauren asked weakly. 'Mel, if Kevin had a sports car he'd catch up with John even if John *had* had an hour's head start.' She buried her face in her hands, trying to keep down a rising feeling of panic. 'If they catch up with him and see him, they'll kill him,' she said hoarsely. 'It's been hours already. They may already have. They may have chased him up some remote mountain road, and . . .'

Mel patted Lauren's shoulder comfortingly. 'Now, don't get upset, sweetheart,' he said. 'I don't think John would get himself trapped like that. He's too smart. But I'll put out a bulletin on your jeep, just in case. If anyone sees it . . .'

'Why don't you put out a bulletin on Kevin Redfern?' Lauren cried. 'Have him stopped. He's the dangerous one!'

'I can't,' Mel said unhappily. 'He didn't do anything to warrant it. Never made any threats or anything. He just said he had to get back to San Francisco in a hurry. Now, why don't you go on back to the lodge and take it easy? If I hear anything . . .'

'No!' Lauren cried. 'I am not going to go back and sit and wait and wait, not knowing what's happened! I'm never going to do that again! If John's going to San Francisco, I am too!' She started for the door.

'Wait a minute,' Mel said, his voice suddenly firm. 'We'll both go. It may not be quite legal, but from what you've told me and what I saw, Kevin Redfern's a suspect in a murder attempt in my jurisdiction. I think maybe I ought to go after him.' He smiled crookedly as Lauren turned and stared at him. 'I can't let you go off alone into something that might be real dangerous. Besides, I've always wanted to see how fast that car of mine can go.'

'Isn't this just as bad as putting out a bulletin on Kevin?' Lauren asked moments later as they tore down the highway in Mel's patrol car, the siren wailing.

'Probably,' Mel replied with a grin, 'but it's a hell of a lot more fun.'

'I suppose it is,' Lauren said, thinking to herself that

Mel Cranston had a side to him that she had never seen before.

To Lauren's surprise, none of the other police vehicles they passed questioned Mel's right to go flying by when he told them he was in pursuit of a fugitive. Nowhere, however, did they see any sign of either her jeep or Kevin Redfern's Maserati. In less time than she would have dreamed possible, they were crossing the Bay Bridge into San Francisco. Suddenly, it occurred to her that she hadn't the slightest idea where in that large city they were going, and she mentioned that fact to Mel.

'We're going to the Redfern mansion,' Mel replied, his eyes glued to the road as he changed lanes of traffic. 'That wimp of a Kevin still lives there, and I expect John would head there, too. It's quite a place. You'll probably see all of it, once you marry John.'

'I . . . yes, I suppose I will,' Lauren said, staring at Mel. He had mentioned her impending marriage to John quite calmly. He glanced over at her and made a wry face.

'Yeah, I know you're going to marry him,' he said. 'I don't like it, but I can see I've got to accept it. I'm just praying everything's going to be all right for you. Damned if I can figure out how John could have made good enough time in the jeep to stay ahead of a Maserati. Neither one can be too far ahead of us.'

Mel calmly threaded his way through the San Francisco traffic, heading up the steep hills to an area of elegant old homes. 'Let me do the talking,' he said to Lauren, as he turned in and stopped at a closed and guarded gate before an immense Victorian mansion. He rolled down his window and held out his police identification. 'I'm looking for a Kevin Redfern,' he barked at the gatekeeper. 'Is he here?'

The gatekeeper bent and peered at Mel. 'Yes, officer,' he replied. 'Who shall I say is here?'

'Don't say a damned thing,' Mel replied. 'The man's a fugitive. A murder suspect. Just let me in and see that the guy at the door doesn't say anything, either.'

The gatekeeper paled. 'Yes, sir! I'll let you in the house myself, sir,' he said. 'That way you won't have to ring the bell.' The man opened the gate and trotted down the drive before them.

'He doesn't seem too surprised that Kevin would be in trouble,' Mel commented drily.

'I still don't see any sign of the jeep,' Lauren said. 'What can have become of John? What are we going to do if he isn't here?'

'I'm going to take Kevin into custody. Then we'll tell the family what we know and play it by ear from there,' Mel said.

'B-but . . . aren't you supposed to have a warrant to arrest a person?' Lauren asked, beginning to feel that perhaps Mel had gone overboard in his zeal to be helpful and protective.

Mel parked the car and looked over at Lauren. 'Not when you're in pursuit of a fugitive,' he said. 'I got the whole story from John, and when I tried to question Kevin this morning he slugged me and then took off. You've never seen me lie before, have you, Lauren? You'd be surprised how good I am when necessary.' With that, Mel got calmly out of the car and strode up to the huge front door of the

Redfern mansion.

Lauren followed, and the gatekeeper quietly opened the door for them to slip inside.

'I'll find out where Mr Kevin is,' he whispered, and Mel nodded in response.

'He must hate "Mr Kevin's" guts,' Mel murmured to Lauren, as the man walked quietly across the marble-floored foyer and disappeared through a doorway.

'Either that or he's going to warn him,' Lauren whispered back. She looked around in the huge, silent foyer and shuddered involuntarily. The walls were a dark, shining wood, hung with gilt-framed pictures of historical battle scenes. On either side of the symmetrical room were two Gothic-arched doorways, the frames heavily ornamented with carved grapevines. From the landing of a curving staircase, a stuffed moose stared balefully down at them. Red velvet curtains covered the window behind the moose. The entire effect was one of a setting for a horror movie. Lauren was just entertaining that thought when a woman's piercing scream coming from a room to the right made her heart stop and the hair on the back of her neck stand up. While her heart stood still, a man's voice, high and raspy, cried out, 'She made me do it! I didn't want to do it! It was all her idea!'

'Put down the gun, Kevin,' said a deep, soft voice.

Lauren turned to Mel, her eyes wide with fear. 'That's John's voice,' she whispered. 'Mel, Kevin's going to . . .' She did not finish, for Mel quietly signalled for her to stand still and then started for the door from which the voices had come, his pistol drawn.

CHAPTER ELEVEN

AFTERWARDS, Lauren remembered the next few minutes as moving in incredibly slow motion. She could not remember breathing or moving at all.

While Mel moved towards the door, a woman cried out, 'Kevin, no! Please, stop and think!'

Then John's voice said, 'Kevin, she's right. Don't be a fool.'

The door Mel reached was slightly ajar. He peered in cautiously, then pushed the door wide and moved into the opening.

'Freeze, Redfern!' he commanded. 'You're covered.'

An instant later, there was simultaneously the sound of scuffling, Mel disappeared from view, and one shot rang out. Then there were two crashes, one of a body falling and one that sounded like glass breaking. 'Got him!' said two male voices at once.

Lauren rushed to the doorway. Mel was crouched on top of Kevin Redfern, fastening his hands behind his back with handcuffs. John was bending over them, watching. When the job was done, he gave Mel a hand in getting up. Then Lauren saw something she had never expected to see. John and Mel embraced each other warmly.

'Great work, Mel,' John said, pumping Mel's hand repeatedly. 'You're better than the US Cavalry used to be at showing up just in the nick of time.

'That was some flying tackle you made, John,' Mel replied. 'You ought to try out for the pros.'

'How did you know . . .' John began, then looked as Mel gestured towards the door.

For the first time, John became aware of Lauren's presence, and as he turned towards her Lauren could see the most wonderful transformation come over his face. From the brittle tension of excitement, it softened, a warm glow of happiness illuminating his smile and spreading to turn the bright blue of his eyes into radiant, translucent pools. Silently, they moved together and held each other close. Then John moved aside, holding Lauren in the crook of his arm.

'Sarah, Father, this is Lauren Stanley,' he said. 'The woman I'm going to marry.'

For the first time, Lauren noticed the other two people in the room. John's stepmother, an attractive woman with silver-blonde hair, elegantly dressed in black, was sitting in a chair across the room, staring numbly into space. At John's introduction the barest flicker of a smile crossed her features. John's father, a somewhat heavier version of John himself, stood up and came towards them.

'How do you do, Lauren,' he said gravely, extending his hand. 'I'm afraid this isn't a very good introduction to the family.' He smiled with that same wry look of amusement that John often had. 'Things can only get better.'

'I'm sure they will,' Lauren replied, taking his hand and squeezing it warmly. She looked over at John's mother. 'Perhaps Mrs Redfern should have a doctor look at her,' she said very softly. 'She may be in shock.' From what John had told her about his stepmother's devotion to Kevin, she knew the woman must have suffered a terrible blow from the events that had just transpired.

'I've already called one, miss,' said a dignified voice behind them, and Lauren turned to see an elderly servant standing there, wringing his hands in distress.

Then there was a commotion in the foyer, and Lauren realised that Mel and Kevin were gone. She followed John and his father to the foyer, where two more police officers were taking charge of Kevin, who was writhing and complaining bitterly. When they had gone, Mel waited behind.

'I'll go on down to the station and see about booking him,' Mel said quietly to John. 'They won't need you for a while. Probably tomorrow morning will be soon enough.'

'Thanks, Mel,' John said, shaking his hand again.

'Mel,' Lauren said, holding out her hand to him, 'I—I don't know how to tell you . . .' She stopped, her voice failing her. What a bittersweet thing it was for Mel to have done his job so well, and yet have lost what he most wanted. Tears filled her eyes, and instead of shaking Mel's hand, she threw her arms around him and hugged him.

'That's all right, Lauren,' Mel said, patting her back comfortingly. 'I understand.' He pulled back and smiled at Lauren, his voice firm although his eyes were misty. 'I always felt bad that there wasn't anything I could do the other time. I'm just awfully glad things turned out the way they did today. As long as you're happy, I'm happy.' He gave them all a little salute, then turned and went out of the door.

'That,' John said in a voice deep with emotion. 'is

one hell of a man.'

Lauren nodded, blinking back her tears. 'He and Paul were in the army together. Paul always said that when the going got rough, there wasn't anyone he'd rather have beside him. I never understood why until today.'

Mr Redfern returned from escorting Kevin to the waiting patrol car. He stood for a moment, staring at Jonathan, his eyes filled with tears. Then the two men embraced. 'Oh, son,' Mr Redfern muttered, 'what you must have gone through.'

Lauren slipped quietly away to find a servant who could direct her to a telephone so that she could call the lodge and tell Isobel and Brian where she was, knowing that by now they must be frantic with worry. She was not very surprised to find that Mel had already called them.

'Did Mel really catch a bad guy?' Brian asked, his little voice awed.

'He really did, love,' Lauren answered. 'John and I will tell you all about it when we get back.' Which, she thought wryly, was going to be a very tricky explanation, the details of which could well be saved for when Brian was older. Then she smiled to herself. John would know how to handle it.

She looked around the ornately elegant salon where she had been taken to make her call and sighed. To think that John had grown up in this place, John who was still wearing the jeans and flannel shirt in which he had gone off to hunt a bear. She was wearing a warm blue sweater and slacks, simple and inexpensive. What would it be like to wear the kind of clothes that would fit with such luxury? She remembered once imagining how John would look in a tuxedo . . .

'Oh, there you are!' John came striding into the room, his head thrown back, looking as much at ease as if he were formally dressed.

Lauren straightened her posture unconsciously. 'I called Isobel and Brian,' she said. 'I didn't have time to tell them where I was going.' She looked down at herself and then back at John. 'I was just thinking that I don't quite measure up to the elegance you're used to.'

John frowned. 'Don't be ridiculous,' he said severely. He cast a scathing glance around the room and shook his head. 'You, my beloved angel, are far more exquisite than anything here could ever be.' He put his arms around Lauren and smiled at her gently. 'There's no love in this place, no real beauty. Perhaps we can bring some here once in a while.' He touched his lips to hers, then pulled her close and laid his cheek against hers. 'I'm afraid we'll have to stay here overnight so that I can take care of some legal details in the morning. My father wants to have dinner with us so he can begin to get acquainted with you . . . actually with both of us, I think. By morning, Sarah should be able to talk to you a little, too. Is that all right? I know this has been a rough day for you.'

'I'll be fine,' Lauren replied, 'as long as I'm with you.' She looked up at John and tilted her head. 'By the way, how on earth did you get here so fast? I can't believe it was in the jeep.

John put on a look of mock surprise. 'Didn't you know the jeep can fly?' he asked. Then he chuckled. 'I left it in Briggsville at the airfield. I took a chance that Redfern Timber still kept a plane there, and they did.'

'Do you mean to tell me that you can fly a plane, too?' Lauren demanded.

'I'm afraid so,' John replied with a grin. Then his face grew serious again. 'I got here over an hour before Kevin did, and had already explained most of what had happened and why to Sarah and my father by the time he got here. He tried to claim that I was lying, but not even Sarah believed him. When he saw that, he began to whine and accuse her of being the cause of all of his troubles. Actually, that's partly true because of the way she spoiled him, but I don't believe that she ever told him to do anything dishonest and I certainly don't believe she suggested he try to get rid of me permanently. She simply thought that if he'd push himself forward, he'd prove to be better than me. Anyway, she cut short his accusations with some of her own, and made it perfectly clear that she wasn't going to take his side this time. That was when Kevin panicked and started brandishing his gun. I don't know if he would have used it, but I'm afraid he might have, as out of control as he seemed to be. Seeing Mel appear in that doorway was one of the pleasantest sights I've ever witnessed. When he told Kevin to freeze, I dived for him. The gun went off and shot out the ceiling light. I think you saw the rest.' He paused and frowned. 'When did you and Mel leave Briggsville? It couldn't have been much more than half an hour between the time Kevin arrived and you and Mel got here.'

'About two hours after Kevin did,' Lauren replied. 'Mel was practically flying. I looked at the speedometer once and it said over a hundred, so I didn't look again.'

'Good lord!' John exclaimed, shaking his head. 'It scares me to think of that kind of speed in traffic on the ground.'

Lauren smiled. 'It was really kind of fun. Besides, it got us here just in the nick of time. It's a good thing we didn't go any slower.'

'I suppose so,' John said. He sighed and held Lauren close. 'This whole day has been too full of close calls to suit me. Damn. I wish we could just be alone for a while, but I think my father needs some company right now. Shall we join him?'

'Of course,' Lauren replied. She held John tightly for a moment. 'John, I do love you so,' she said softly. Then she released him and let him lead her through a seemingly endless series of hallways to a warm, book-lined room where a small table had been set for three.

The three spent a long evening talking, Theodore Redfern eager to learn all of the details of his son's long absence and equally eager to find out about his future daughter-in-law. The fact that he would also acquire a grandson delighted him.

'I've waited far too long for that already,' he said. 'I need someone to take to the zoo.' He leaned back and smiled that familiar, amused little smile. 'It may seem strange for me to say this tonight, but I feel better right now than I have in a long, long time. It hurt so, when Jon and I grew apart, but I didn't know what to do. Then, when he was gone, I felt as if a part of me was missing too.' He paused, blinking rapidly, then took a deep breath and smiled again. 'I'm twice blessed to have him back, so happy in the love of a beautiful woman. What do you two children plan to do when you leave here tomorrow? Jon says you plan to be married as soon as possible.'

'Well,' John said thoughtfully, looking over at Lauren, 'I think we'll fly back to Briggsville, stop by the lodge, and then, if it isn't too late, we'll drive on over to Reno and get married. That is, if Lauren wants to do that.'

'Tomorrow?' Lauren stared at him, her pulse quickening. 'That sounds absolutely heavenly. You bet I want to!' She turned to Theodore Redfern. 'I wish you and Mrs Redfern could be there, though.'

'Let me know when you're sure and I'll fly up,' he said. 'I'd love to be with you. I think it would do Sarah good to come, too, if the doctor says she's up to it. She's been quite disillusioned with Kevin in the past year, and she needs something positive to focus on now. Well, perhaps we should call it a night. Jon will want to get his ordeal over with as early as possible tomorrow so he can get on to more pleasant things.'

John was silent for a long time after his father had left the room. At last he looked over at Lauren and said softly, 'I never knew until today how much I loved my father and how much he cared for me. It's hard to think of everything that's happened as a blessing in disguise, especially considering what poor Kevin's facing now, but it almost seems to be. I was wondering . . .' he paused and looked directly at Lauren, 'would you mind very much if I didn't change my name, after all?'

Lauren shook her head. 'I was thinking that perhaps you shouldn't,' she replied. 'Your father might be hurt if you did. Besides, I can still call you John, without an H.'

'That's what I think, too,' John said. He stood up and held out his arms to Lauren. 'Come to me, my love, and give me a nice, proper kiss so that I don't go crazy overnight from wanting you. Then I'll have Tilford show you to your room. Only one more night, and you'll be mine.'

Shortly after one o'clock the next afternoon, the sign for Stoney Creek Lodge came into view. Jon turned the car he had rented, for fear that the jeep might not make it to Reno and back, on to the road to the lodge, then pulled to the side and stopped.

'Why are we stopping here?' Lauren asked.

'Because,' Jon said, turning to take her into his arms, 'before we are assaulted by Brian and Isobel, I wanted to tell you something, and to do this.' He lowered his mouth to hers, then gathered her close, his kiss deepening so passionately that Lauren melted against him, her arms going around him to revel in the strong, hard strength that was at once so powerful and so gentle. She sighed as his lips left her mouth to nibble a trail of little kisses towards her ear.

'I love you, Jonathan Redfern,' she said softly.

'I love you too, angel,' he said, pulling his head back so that he could look into her eyes. 'It seems like such a long time since we could be alone and I could hold you and kiss you and tell you that I loved you. That's what I wanted to tell you. That I love you more with every passing day, even though each day it doesn't seem possible my heart could hold more love for you.'

Lauren took Jon's face between her hands, her eyes

bright with tears of happiness. 'I've always heard that true loves grows day by day. I'm sure that ours will keep on growing forever.' She pulled him close and covered his face with kisses, only stopping when Jon put her firmly from him and started the car again.

'Desist, woman,' he said. 'I've got to hold out a few more hours until our wedding night. Now, let's see how fast we can get the troops organised. Dad and Sarah are meeting us at five o'clock.'

Jon insisted that Brian come with them on their trip to Reno so that he would know their marriage was something real, and not a mysterious event that took place far away. With Brian and Mr and Mrs Redfern at their sides, Jon and Lauren exchanged their vows in a small wedding chapel, then drove back to Stoney Creek Lodge alone while an excited Brian flew back to Briggsville with his new grandparents in the Redfern company plane. The three of them then drove to the lodge with Mel. Isobel had produced a beautiful wedding cake while they were gone, and the guests at the lodge joined in the celebration of the marriage as if they had known the newlyweds all their lives.

It was late that evening when Jon and Lauren were finally able to be alone in their apartment, Isobel having tactfully taken a still very excited Brian to spend the night on a cot in her room.

'I think this is where I'm supposed to say "Alone at last",' Jon said, closing the apartment door firmly and locking it. He held out his arms. 'Come to me, my adorable angel,' he said.

Lauren walked to him and stood in the circle of his arms, gazing into his eyes, her heart filled with happiness. She put her arms around him and laid her cheek against his chest. 'I'm still having trouble believing it's really happened,' she said. 'Only yesterday . . .'

'Hush, Mrs Redfern,' Jon said sternly. 'This is today. In fact, it is tonight. And tonight . . .' he bent suddenly and swept Lauren into his arms, his eyes alight with delighted mischief as he smiled down at her '. . . tonight we are going to concentrate on only one thing. We are going to make love, and make love, and make love.'

'What a wonderful plan,' Lauren said, gazing into the vivid blue warmth of Jon's eyes. 'I've wanted you all evening, so much that it hurts.'

Jon smiled and shook his head. 'There were times I didn't think I'd make it through that party, pleasant though it was.' He picked Lauren up and carried her into their bedroom. As if she were as delicate as the angel he thought her, he laid her on the bed and with eager but gentle hands helped her remove the soft blue silken dress she wore. He quickly removed most of his own clothing, then curled his long body beside Lauren, feasting his eyes on her and murmuring words of such adoration that she smiled and said teasingly, 'I do believe you'll have me quite vain if you keep that up.'

'I'm already quite vain,' he replied, bending to tease her soft bosom with his tongue, 'to think that such a lovely creature would want to be my wife.' In only a few more moments, the barrier of clothing was gone from them both. Jon stretched out against Lauren and sighed deeply. 'I've wanted to do this since the first moment I saw you,' he whispered in her ear. 'It's a good thing you didn't know it at the time. You'd never have brought me home with you.'

'Don't be too sure of that,' Lauren replied, laughing delightedly when Jon gave her bare bottom a playful pinch.

'Wicked woman,' he said, enfolding her in his arms and throwing one long leg across her. 'Just for that, I think I shall kiss you until you beg for mercy.' He lowered his mouth to hers, touching her lips softly at first, then suddenly bearing down with a possessive passion that took her breath away. All of the anxiety and fatigue of the past days was swept away before an excitement that sent her soaring, weightless in a world where only Jon's closeness existed, only his body against hers, his hands caressing, searching, and finding. She revelled in the gentle touch of his hands against her bare skin, a touch that sent signals of fire radiating through her, as if her skin wanted to help confirm that the wild happiness she felt inside was not only a dream. She pressed eagerly against the hands that gently cupped and kneaded her breasts. When Jon's lips wandered slowly down her throat, she heard herself sighing deeply in anticipation of the moment when they took possession of the rosy peaks that his fingers had teased to eager hardness. The gentle tugging sent cascades of desire rushing through her. She dug her fingers into his shoulders, pulling him closer. She moved her body against his, telling him that there was more than she wanted, so much more. She loved him with all her heart, and she wanted to belong to him, completely, from this moment on.

'My precious angel,' Jon murmured, raising his head, his eyes dark and somnolent with his own strong desire. He rose to take possession of her,

Lauren's body beneath his, his arms moulding her against him, his mouth devouring hers again, thrusting his strong male hardness into her carefully and deeply. When Lauren responded with a soft little moan of pleasure and arched to meet him, he quickened the pace of his movements, lifting his head to smile at her in delight as she told him with sounds of pure joy that she was soaring with him into that unique world of shared ecstasy that only lovers know.

Lauren clung to Jon, watching his smile, losing herself completely in sensations so heavenly that she could scarcely believe she had not left the earth for some rendezvous among the clouds. Then, just when she thought she could go no farther, there came a sudden crescendo, a leaping to a still higher plane. Jon made a deep, male sound of triumphant joy. Together they hovered, the world spinning giddily below, then slowly, like birds descending from one cloud to another, returned to earth and lay still in each other's arms.

At last Jon roused himself and moved to hold Lauren against his shoulder. 'You may think this is a little strange,' he said, caressing her hair back with his hand and smiling at her lovingly, 'but I just thought of the last verse of our song.'

'I don't think it's strange at all,' Lauren said, catching his hand and kissing it. 'I was just thinking that I wished I could describe how I felt right now. But words don't come to me like that. Tell me what you thought of.'

'All right.' Very softly, Jon sang the first part of the song:

'In mountains cold with lonely paths,

Where fear still followed sorrow.
The light of love came into view,
My heart longed for tomorrow.
I sent it forth with warmth and hope,
To face its certain capture.
And find a home where love could grow,
For all the days ever after.'

Then he kissed Lauren's lips and concluded:

'It found the treasure it had sought,
In mountains warm and green.
A love more sweet and beautiful,
Than any I had dreamed.'

'It is that way, isn't it?' Lauren said when he had finished. 'Better than any dream could possibly be.'

Jon nodded. 'And it will stay that way. For all the days ever after.'